CHOOSING HAPPILY EVER AFTER

ELENA AITKEN

Also by Elena Aitken

Ever After

The Springs Series

His to Tame

His to Seek

Hers for the Season

Bears of Grizzly Ridge: Books 1-4

Bears of Grizzly Ridge: Books 5-8

Halfway Series

Halfway to Nowhere

Halfway in Between

Halfway to Christmas

Chapter One

SHE WAS GORGEOUS. All dressed in white, of course. The veil covered her face, but there was no doubt that beneath the gauzy film was the hint of a smile while she tried to bite back the tears that threatened to spill down her cheeks despite the bride's insistence earlier that she *"absolutely will not cry. I'm just not a crier."*

Hope Turner had seen it a million times before. And they almost always cried.

At least a little.

"Are you ready?" she asked the bride, who clutched her father's arm tightly. "Just like we practiced."

"Only this time it's for real."

Hope nodded. "It is."

She'd also seen this a million times. A bride and groom who laughed and joked their way through the rehearsal the night before and then completely came undone at the actual ceremony the moment they realized that it was, in fact, *real.*

"And you *are* ready," she added. "It's going to be great." The bride nodded and looked straight ahead. That was Hope's cue.

She whipped out her phone, which also served as a control station for basically everything, and tapped a button. A moment later, the traditional wedding march—the bride's choice, not hers— filled the outdoor ceremony space Hope had dubbed Riverbend, due to the fact that it was, in fact, in the bend of the river. She had her pick of perfect ceremony sites on Ever After Ranch, but this was her favorite.

Hope stepped back and let the bride's father lead her down the grassy aisle toward her groom, whom, she was absolutely certain, would also be dabbing his eyes through the entire ceremony.

The bride made it safely to the end of the aisle, hugged her father, and took her groom's hand as the ceremony began. There was a time when there was nothing Hope enjoyed more than listening to the couple recite their vows. After all, it didn't get any more romantic. But lately, there hadn't been time to enjoy the details of the beautiful weddings she put on. There was just too much to do.

Which was why, as soon as the officiant began speaking, Hope scurried away in the golf cart that she'd recently started using to get from place to place around the ranch, back up to the Barn, where the reception was to be held to double-check with the catering staff that everything was set up. Just as she'd instructed, champagne was poured and ready to go on trays by the entrance. The servers stood by with canapés to keep guests entertained while the newlywed couple went for a few photographs around the property.

Hope did a quick spin of the reception space, a refurbished barn that was her pride and joy and also the reason that her business was booming in the last few years. It was rustic elegance that spoke to the dreams of many engaged couples. It didn't hurt that it had the capacity for large gatherings, and a wedding coordinator who could handle anything that was thrown at her. She'd come a long way from the little girl who, along with her twin sister, used to beg her parents to help with the few weddings that they'd host on the lawns of their sprawling mountain property. Back then, it hadn't been a business. Not really. Just a little bit of *fun money*, her mom used to call it. Something to do when things were slow with the ranching business, or more usual, when there was a special request to hold an event on their property. The Turner ranch had always been gorgeous.

And Hope had seen the potential. Of course, not even her grandest dreams could have prepared her for how successful Ever After Ranch would be and just how busy she'd find herself in such a short time.

Satisfied that the reception was ready, Hope gave a few final instructions to the catering staff, who she already knew didn't need them, and raced back down to the ceremony space just as the officiant was declaring the happy couple husband and wife.

Perfect timing.

She quickly pressed another button on her phone and new music played over the speakers. The crowd cheered and the bride and groom danced down the aisle with their arms in the air, and ever so slightly red eyes, just as Hope predicted.

It wasn't until hours later, after the photographs, the speeches, and dinner, with the guests all happily dancing the night away on the hardwood floors of the barn, that Hope had a minute to hop in her cart and head back to the ceremony site to clean up any garbage that guests had left behind, pack up the speakers and sound system, and take care of anything else that couldn't be left out in the elements.

The stars and the moon lit up the night sky and in desperate need to sit down, Hope gave in and did just that. She tipped her head up and let herself take it all in.

When was the last time she'd stopped and just looked up?

She couldn't remember. But that's what it was like to build

a business. Exhausting. Which would explain why she could barely keep her eyes open. She felt it deep in her bones. An overwhelming exhaustion. It was different than her usual tiredness. Of course, she was taking on more bookings than ever before. Maybe it was time to bring on an assistant.

Or her sister.

Hope almost laughed out loud at herself. There was no way. Nevertheless, it was worth a shot. Well, it was worth *another shot*. Still chuckling, she pulled out her cell phone and pressed the button for her twin sister.

"It's late on a Saturday," Faith answered. "Shouldn't you be busy perpetuating the myth of happy ever after and charging tens of thousands of dollars for it while you're at it?"

Hope shook her head and rolled her eyes. "Hi to you, too, sis." Where Hope was a die-hard romantic, which had led to the idea of her business in the first place, her twin sister, although identical in appearance, couldn't be more opposite in her feelings about love and marriage. "So I was thinking…" *Might as well get right to the point.*

"No."

"You don't even know what I'm going to ask." She groaned and moved the phone to her other ear. "At least wait until I—"

"You're going to ask me to come home to Glacier Falls and run the ranch with you," her sister said matter-of-factly. "Just like you always do when I answer the phone at eleven p.m. on a Saturday night. And just like it always is, the answer is no. I hate that shit, Hope. You know that."

She did.

"But you love me."

"I do."

"So do it for me. To help me out." She knew it was pointless, but she tried anyway. "Besides, it will be fun. We can be the wedding sisters again, like when we were kids."

It was one of Hope's favorite memories, when their mother

would dress them up in frilly dresses and give them baskets of flower petals to throw on the newly married couples. Guests had loved the identical blonde-haired, little girls. Hope had loved it too. Faith, not so much. But even so, there had been a handful of times when Hope had managed to convince her sister from time to time to dress up and reenact their own weddings, taking turns with who got to be the bride and who had to play the groom.

"If you're trying to convince me, that's the wrong way to do it." Faith laughed and then added, "Seriously though, if you need help, Hope, hire someone. Because as much as I love you, I'll be staying in the city. Sorry." She actually did sound a little sorry this time. "Put an ad on the town's Facebook page or something. You'll get someone."

"Yeah, maybe. But hey, you can't blame a girl for trying. Let's talk tomorrow, okay?" Hope smiled into the phone. Distance and lifestyle may separate them, but they were still close. "Love you."

"Love you too, Hope," Faith said. "And Hope? Get some sleep. You sound exhausted."

She hung up the phone and tucked it away before going to gather up the rest of the things that couldn't wait until morning. Hope fell heavy into her golf cart and checked the time. There was still at least two hours before she could announce last call. And then she got to start the process of cleaning up.

Hope closed her eyes, but only for a moment. She couldn't risk falling asleep. Maybe Faith was right; maybe she really should hire someone. She was exhausted already and the wedding season was only just beginning. Before she could talk herself out of it, Hope opened the Facebook app on her phone and typed up a quick help wanted ad.

After all, it couldn't hurt.

. . .

"I'm not saying it's not good to have you back…"

"It's just strange," Levi Langdon finished for his cousin, Logan. "I get it. It is strange." Levi lifted the bottle to his lips and let the cold beer slide down his throat. As strange as it was to be back in his hometown after almost ten years, it also felt good. Really good. Like putting on an old sweater. Or in this case, an old pair of work boots to help Logan out on his family ranch. The ranch he'd grown up on and couldn't wait to leave.

"But I'm not complaining." Logan grinned. "I've missed you and it was good to be out there today. When was the last time we rode the fence line like that together?"

Levi chuckled and shook his head because they both knew the answer. He'd been twenty years old, Logan a year ahead of him, and they'd both been caught drinking Logan's dad's beers. Both were of legal drinking age in Canada, not that it mattered to Uncle Harold. They were *his* beers. An already hard man got even harder when someone took his beers. Especially his dead sister's kid. For whatever reason, Uncle Harold had a special place in his heart for Levi. And it wasn't a good one.

Their punishment had been to ride the fence line and repair some downed wire in the middle of the night. Of course, Levi's punishment had also included a punch in the face that only narrowly missed breaking his nose, but he'd sported the shiner for weeks. It was the last time they'd rode the fence together, because it had also been the last time Levi had spent the night under his uncle's roof.

He'd had enough. Besides, he was already living on borrowed time on the Langdon ranch. A fact Uncle Harold had no trouble reminding him of on a regular basis. He should have left years ago but he'd been trying to save up enough money to get an apartment in the city. Or at least enough to set him up. But leaving early couldn't hurt. Hell, it would probably hurt a whole lot less.

At least that's what he'd thought at the time.

Levi blinked hard and shook his head. Coming back to Glacier Falls was hard enough. He didn't need to relive every goddamn heartbreaking moment.

"Right." Logan lifted his own beer, obviously remembering that night as well. "Hey, about all of that." He wiped his mouth on the back of his sleeve. "I'm really sorry that my dad treated you like that back then. I don't—"

"Want you to worry about it," Levi answered for him. "It wasn't your fault and you can't own the actions of your parents. Hell, we'd both be in trouble if that were the case." He hadn't known his dad, but all accounts were that he was a deadbeat asshole who'd left his mom knocked up and alone. Levi didn't even know what his last name was, having been given his mother's family name. And it didn't matter; he'd never cared to know who the man was.

Levi had nothing but love for his mother, what he could remember of her anyway. She'd died when he was only ten and he'd gone to live with her brother's family in Glacier Falls. It had been a mixed blessing. Logan had been a cousin, best friend, and brother all rolled into one. Katie had been like a little sister to him, and Auntie Deb had done her best to love and protect young Levi from the unexplainable anger of her husband that only got worse the older he got.

Leaving them had been just as hard as it had been easy leaving Uncle Harold. But now Uncle Harold was gone, having died three months earlier from a heart attack. And Levi was back.

"Still," Logan said. "I'm sorry he was such a dick to you. He never could explain it, and I know you don't want to hear it, or you wouldn't believe it anyway, but he really wasn't like that with Katie and me."

"That I do believe." He took another long pull from his beer. "It doesn't matter now," he said again, meaning it. "I'm looking forward to catching up with you all. I've missed all of you."

"Just us?"

If he hadn't been on the other side of the shop, Levi likely would have punched his cousin or at least given him a shove. He hadn't even been back for a full twenty-four hours. There was no need to stir the pot. Logan knew damn well that his family wasn't the only thing he'd missed about Glacier Falls. Far from it.

"How is Hope?"

Hope Turner, the love of Levi's young life. Or at least he'd thought she was at the time. With her long blonde hair and innocent blue eyes, he'd been completely wrapped around her little finger. He would have done anything for that girl.

Except stay in town.

As much as he loved her, he knew in his heart that if he stayed, Uncle Harold would slowly beat down his spirit—and his body—and in a small town, there was nowhere else to go. Leaving her had been the hardest thing he'd ever done and as much as he wanted to, he couldn't ask her to go with him, because he knew her heart was in Glacier Falls. She loved her small town, and more than that, the ranch she grew up on. She was never leaving. He knew it just like he also knew if he asked her, it would break her heart to have to choose. So he'd let her go.

To his credit, Logan didn't make a smart-ass comment the way Levi was so sure he would. Instead, he slowly put his beer down on the workbench he sat on and crossed his arms. "Ten years, and you've never once asked about her."

Levi nodded. It was true.

"That must mean you're finally over her."

He laughed but didn't answer right away. There would be a part of him that was never completely over Hope Turner. But he'd been a kid the last time he'd seen her. A lot changed in ten years. "It's been a long time."

"That didn't answer my question." Logan raised an eyebrow at him before hopping down off the bench and moving across the shop to the beer fridge. They hadn't even been in the house yet, a fact Levi felt a little guilty for. But it was late and he hadn't told anyone he was coming. He'd surprised Logan by joining him in the field earlier, but it was getting late now. He'd just have to surprise Aunt Deb and Katie in the morning. He accepted another beer from his cousin but paused before opening it when Logan said, "Hope's killing it with her business. Turned her family ranch into a wedding venue, of all things."

Levi laughed and shook his head but he wasn't surprised. Ever since they were kids, Hope talked about the few weddings they held out on their property. She'd always been a hopeless romantic. "I'm glad it's working out," he said. "But I'm not surprised. She always knew exactly what she wanted."

Again, Logan raised his eyebrow, but didn't say anything. "She must be doing even better than last year." He handed Levi his cell phone. "She just posted on Facebook that she's looking to hire some help."

Levi took the phone without trying to look too eager. He was pretty sure he failed, but he couldn't help it. Talking about Hope had his pulse racing. He'd managed to avoid her on social media all these years, largely because he wasn't on any social media, but it didn't mean he hadn't thought about how easy it would be to see what she was up to. Was she married? Did she have kids? Was she happy? All things he could know if he'd joined the Facebook phenomenon. Which was precisely why he didn't. But that didn't stop him from grabbing his cousin's phone and looking at the familiar, yet different, beautiful face on the tiny screen.

Hope Turner.

She looked the same, but also so different. She definitely wasn't the innocent girl he'd left. Although she still had the sweet look of complete trust in her eyes, there was also something else in her expression. Something deeper.

Levi forced himself to look away from her profile picture and scroll down on the screen to the post Logan was referring to.

Help wanted: General handyman, jack of all trades. Must love love.

He couldn't help but laugh. She was still a hopeless romantic. Some things never changed.

What if there were a few more things that hadn't changed?

Levi looked up at Logan, who clearly saw the expression on his cousin's face. "Looking for a job, are you, cuz?"

Chapter Two

FAITH TURNER EXHALED SLOWLY and rolled herself to the edge of the bed, careful not to wake Noah. She hadn't meant to spend the night. Not at all. It was a rule she never broke.

Except when she did.

Like when Noah made her come as hard as he had the night before. Twice.

Her body was deliciously sore. The man really did know his way around a woman's body. More specifically—*her* body. And she was not complaining at all. It was too bad she was going to have to break up with him.

She tiptoed her way across his bedroom, picking up various articles of clothing as she went. The trail led her out to the living room of his one-bedroom condo. She paused to take in the view of the downtown core and river. He had an amazing view and with the sun rising over the river in vibrant shades of pinks, purples, and oranges, it was almost enough to get her to change her mind, turn around and crawl back into bed so she could enjoy the view from the comfort of his bed—and his arms. It was tempting. Very tempting. Especially because she knew that cuddle would result in a whole lot more than cuddling.

Her body tingled with the promise of what it would mean.

But no. She had to stay strong. She'd already broken her overnight rule too many times. And if she stayed, it might turn into all day and then another night, and the last thing she could afford to do was be late for work on Monday morning.

And considering Noah Simmons was her superior, that was definitely not a good idea.

She sighed and turned away from the view before tugging her dress over her head and moving through the room to the door.

It was also just one more reason why she had to break up with him. Dating your boss was never a good idea, which was why Faith made it a point never to do it.

Except when she did.

Not that she was even supposed to be dating Noah. She'd told him, no strings. Nothing serious. Just sex.

And that was the main reason why she had to break up with him. No matter how many times she'd told him she wasn't interested in a relationship, or anything serious, he insisted on asking her out on real dates. Faith didn't *do* dinner or movies or the theater or anything else with a man. It only led to one thing—relationships. And relationships only led to drama and hurt feelings, and that was the last thing she needed.

She didn't have the time or patience for love and romance and relationships or any of that bullshit. She'd happily leave that kind of stuff to Hope.

Just thinking about her twin sister reminded Faith about the conversation they'd had the night before. It wasn't unusual for them to have late-night chats. Especially with Hope staying up to all hours during the wedding season. But it was unusual to hear her sister sound so tired. It was concerning. Maybe it was twin intuition, but Faith couldn't help but feel like something was wrong with Hope.

With the majority of her things tucked under her arm, Faith opened the door and slid out into the hallway as quietly as she could before putting her heels on, tugging her long tangled blonde hair into a ponytail and making her way down the hall. It was still early enough on a Sunday morning that she wasn't likely to run into too many people. Not that she cared. It wasn't the first time she did the *walk of shame*. Man, she hated that phrase—after all, why should she feel any shame at all for being a woman who knew exactly what she wanted and what she didn't want?

She pushed her way out into the cool early morning air and dug her cell phone from her purse. She wasn't worried about calling too early. If she knew Hope, she'd already be at the barn, pulling down the wedding decorations from the night before. She was a workaholic, of that there was no doubt.

Sure enough, her sister answered in only two rings.

"You're up early," Hope said as a way of greeting. "Whose bed are you sneaking out of?" Faith laughed. Her twin knew her well. "And do I get to meet this one?"

"You know you don't." Faith shook her head and glanced behind her in the direction of Noah's condo. She couldn't be one hundred percent sure, but it sure as hell looked like his beautiful naked body standing in the picture window, watching her go. She waved, just in case it was him, turned and kept walking. "I'm going to end it right away." She tried to sound confident, but the words stuck in her throat a little. She liked Noah. More than any of the other men who'd come and gone through her life.

And that was one more—very important—reason why she had to break it off. It was one thing for him to get too serious, but when *she* started to develop feelings, that's when the alarm bells really started to go off.

"I don't know why you fight it so hard, Faith." She could almost see her sister shaking her head across the phone line. "You could be really happy if you just let yourself."

"I'm plenty happy." She plucked the parking ticket off the windshield of her car and opened the door, throwing the ticket on the seat next to her. She really should stop parking in short-term parking. "Besides, you're one to talk. You're so busy giving everyone else their happily ever after, but I don't see you going after yours, sis. You're not getting any younger, you know?"

Hope laughed. "Don't I know it? I'm feeling every minute of my age today," she said. "I can't believe how tired I am these days. It's strange. Are you supposed to feel so damn old when you're thirty?"

There it was again, the flicker of worry. "Have you seen a doctor?"

"I don't need a doctor." Hope dismissed her. "I need help around here. You know, I could really use——"

"An employee?" Faith cut her off swiftly as she transferred the call to her hands-free and started the engine. "Because unless you're on your deathbed, there is no way you're going to catch me playing the role of happily-ever-after wedding conductor." She laughed. "You know me better than that. I'd rather——"

"Yeah, yeah. I get it. But it wouldn't hurt if you came back to visit. I miss you."

That softened her. "I miss you, too." Faith pulled out into the still empty downtown street. She lived only about ten minutes away, but unlike Noah, her salary definitely didn't afford her a downtown, river view in a booming city like Calgary. "Are you coming into the city soon?"

"I might. But you know I was thinking you could come here."

Faith knew exactly what her sister meant. She could count

on one hand how many times she'd been back to the ranch since their parents died. It wasn't because she didn't love Hope, not at all. But after the funeral, it was too hard to go back. There were too many memories. Most of them good, of course. But it was easier to lose herself in work and stay in the city and then it just became easier to stay away. Especially when Hope's wedding business took off. Weddings, and all the lovey-dovey bullshit that went with them, made her unreasonably uncomfortable. Still, it made her feel like an asshole that she didn't visit her sister because of her own issues.

"I'll think about it." It was a lie, and they both knew it. "How was the wedding last night? Did you get any sleep?"

For the next few minutes, Hope told her all the details that she never wanted to know about the event the night before. She could hear the excitement in her sister's voice when she mentioned different details, and for Hope's sake, she tried her best to sound somewhat interested.

"But did you get any rest?" Faith really was worried about her.

"Not much," Hope admitted. "But I did take your suggestion and posted a job opening on Facebook. So maybe I'll get a little help around here after all."

"Good. You need it. You're probably up on a ladder right now cleaning up, aren't you?"

Hope laughed. "Well, I'm not on a ladder," she admitted. "But I am…"

Faith waited a beat. "You're what?" she finally prompted. "Hope? You're what?"

She was about to check to see whether the call had disconnected, when her sister's voice came over the line again. This time it had a breathy, airy quality, as if she didn't realize she was speaking out loud. "I'm…I'm…Levi?"

Levi Langdon? The one and only man who'd ever broken her sister's heart? That Levi?

"Levi? What about him?" Faith asked cautiously. "Hope? Are you okay?"

"I'm...Levi Langdon? Is that you?"

Oh shit.

That was really the only thing that she could think at the realization that it was *that* Levi. And he was clearly back from wherever the hell he'd gone all those years ago when he crushed Hope's heart. But a moment later, when Hope muttered something about having to go before disconnecting the call altogether, there were definitely a few more choice words that came to Faith's mind.

"Levi Langdon? Is that you?"

It was a reflex, and maybe one Hope should have thought about a little bit more, but the moment she saw the familiar yet different face of her first—okay, only—love, Hope disconnected her phone call, tucked her cell into her back pocket and ran toward the man she hadn't seen in almost ten years.

It wasn't until she'd wrapped her arms around him and was hugging him that she realized that pretty much any other reaction would have been a better choice. But by then it was too late. Besides, he was wrapping his strong arms around her —*had they gotten stronger?*—and was hugging her back.

Damn. He smelled good. Really good. Like salty air and the ocean, but also of something more familiar. Something more...Levi.

"Hey," he said. His voice was the same, too. Maybe a little deeper, a little rougher, but the same. "It's good to see you, Hope."

Hearing him say her name broke whatever spell she'd been under that had allowed her to let down her guard too easily and so completely. Hope pulled back abruptly, but not before taking one last inhale. She stepped back, and then a bit farther, needing a safe distance between them, lest she throw herself into his arms as if she were an eighteen-year-old kid again.

"It's…" *What? It was what? Good to see him?* Was it? She didn't know. It had been so long. *Too* long. Hope, in fact, didn't know what it was. Finally she settled on something safe. "It's unexpected to see you."

Well, maybe it wasn't that *safe.* She shook her head and tried again. "What are you doing here, Levi?"

It was a fair question. More than fair considering the last time he'd seen her, he'd told her that he was leaving Glacier Falls and was never coming back. And more than that, he was going alone. Without her.

And then he'd left her staring after him, tears streaming down her face and her heart breaking in her chest.

"I know I'm the last person that you expected to see, Hope, and I'm…" He ran a hand over his face and ruffled his hair before shaking his head. "I'm sorry."

Something about the way he said the word rubbed her the wrong way. She took another step back and crossed her arms. "You're sorry?"

"I am."

"For what exactly?"

He must have sensed the anger that had sparked to life in her because he took his own careful step backward before saying, "For dropping in on you like this without warning." His lips twitched up a little bit into a smile that she really didn't want to think was sexy, but dammit, it was. "For leaving you the way I did." The smile fell off his face at the exact moment her stomach clenched tight. "For not calling," he continued, but she no longer wanted the apology. Hope shook her head, but Levi continued, "For more things then I could possibly fit into this apology. But still, I'm sorry, Hope."

She squeezed her eyes shut, but only for a moment. Just long enough to let her muscles in her stomach relax. She took a deep breath and exhaled slowly. She wasn't the same girl she was all those years ago. She'd come along way. A *real* long way. A lot had changed.

But the one thing that hadn't changed was that Hope didn't hold a grudge. There were still a lot of feelings surrounding Levi Langdon, most of which she couldn't process at that moment. But seeing him again felt good. *Really* good. She opened her eyes and smiled. "Okay."

"Okay?"

"Well, not really," she admitted. "But that apology will do. For now," she added with a wink. "But seriously, why are you here?"

Instead of answering the question, Levi looked around the barn. In its current state of dishevel, it didn't look like much. But it was Hope's pride and joy and she couldn't help but feel a surge of pride for what she'd created all on her own. "This is impressive," he said after a moment. "I can't believe what you've done here, Hope. And Logan told me all about how busy you were." He looked back at her, his green eyes looking straight through her the way they always had. "You've done really well for yourself."

She nodded. "You should have seen it last night. It was incredible."

"I bet it was," he said softly. "Everything you do is incredible." He took a step toward her and for the briefest of moments, with the way he was looking at her, his scent still filling her senses, it was as if she'd been transported back in time. Feelings she'd thought were long dead crashed through her, threatening to knock her off-balance.

Before he could notice the way he affected her, Hope took a breath and turned around to face the table she'd been clearing before he'd walked in. She just needed a moment to pull herself together. Her cell phone chirped in her pocket but she ignored it.

"Hope, I really wanted to—"

"I was really sorry to hear—"

She turned around and laughed. "You go first."

"No," he insisted. "Ladies first. You were sorry to hear what?"

"About your uncle," she finished lamely because she knew it was a ridiculous thing to say to Levi, of all people. He'd never had a good relationship with Harold Langdon. And that was putting it mildly.

"You know I'm not." He shook his head with a humorless chuckle. "Well, that's not entirely true. I'm sorry for Logan and Katie. And of course Aunt Debbie. His death was a shock to them all."

Hope nodded. "Is that why you're back?"

"Yes and no." He looked as if he wanted to cross the distance between them, but thankfully held himself back. He was already too close, as far as Hope was concerned. There were way too many feelings flying around between the two of them. If he got any closer, she didn't know whether she'd be able to handle it. Besides that, her skin still burned from where she'd touched him earlier. How was it that the man could still have such an effect on her after all these years? It wasn't fair. Not even a little bit. "I've been out working on the coast," Levi continued. "On a fishing boat."

"A boat?" Hope didn't even pretend to hide her shock. Not once had Levi expressed any interest in boats. He'd loved the land. The horses, ranching, growing things. Besides the fact that he'd lived on the coast in Vancouver with his mother before moving into the mountains when he was a kid, he'd never really expressed any real interest in the ocean. Except for the time when she'd told him how she'd never seen it. Never touched the salty water with her own hands. He'd talked then about how amazing it was, how vast and powerful. He'd also promised her that he'd show the ocean to her one day. That he'd take her himself. That he'd take her anywhere she wanted to go.

But that had been a long time ago. A lot had changed.

Hope swallowed back the memory. "I wouldn't have expected that."

Levi blushed and ducked his head a little.

Did he remember that long-ago promise, too?

Did it matter?

"It's been good money," he continued. "But the boat I've been working on is out on dry dock right now for some repairs so I thought I'd take a bit of time off instead of jumping on with a different crew. And since it's been a few years since I've been back, I thought maybe I'd come check in."

A few years?

Hope swallowed hard. Her cell phone chirped in her pocket again, but this time needing something to distract her, she reached in and pulled it out.

LEVI LANGDON!? WTF?!

She laughed out loud. She shouldn't have been surprised that Faith would be freaking out. She scrolled down to the latest text.

Are you okay?

She typed in a quick response.

All good. I'll call later.

. . .

It wouldn't be enough to satisfy her sister's nosiness, but at least it would prevent her from calling emergency services to come and check on her.

"Everything okay?" Levi watched her carefully. He nodded to the phone in her hand as she tucked it away again.

"Fine. It's just Faith."

"How's Faith?" He smiled. Faith and Levi had gotten along like brother and sister. Hope hadn't been the only one affected by Levi's departure. Only where Hope was brokenhearted, Faith had been pissed off. *Really* pissed off. She still didn't know all the details, but there'd been a story about Faith confronting Logan, Levi's cousin, in a rather dramatic fashion, demanding answers about where Levi had gone. The two of them had always been a bit of a firestorm, arguing just for the sake of it, but stories had circulated around town about the showdown the two of them had that particular day in the middle of the grocery store. Hope had never asked her sister exactly what had gone down, but she did know that Faith hadn't gotten anything more out of Logan. She knew where Levi wasn't, and that was the only thing that mattered.

"Why are you here, Levi?" Hope crossed her arms and looked him in the eye. "Really? Why are you here?"

Levi could have lied to her. Or made up something else about what had brought him out to her barn so early on a Sunday morning. Or he could have told her the truth he could hardly face himself—that he couldn't stay away. Any of those options would have been safer than what he was about to say. But Levi wasn't known for taking the safe option, so he said, "I came for the job."

Her bravado wavered, but only slightly. In fact, if he hadn't been paying very close attention to every single thing about her, he might not have noticed the way her eyes blinked a fraction of a second too long, or the way her knee buckled the tiniest bit before straightening again.

She was strong. Stronger than he remembered. Not that she'd been weak or fragile in any way, but Hope had always been the slightly softer of the twins, where Faith had a hard edge running through her.

She shook her head a little. "The what?"

"The job," he said. "You posted on Facebook. Last night? You posted—"

"I know what I posted," she interrupted him. "But what do you mean, you're here for the job? You just finished telling me that you're working on the coast." She dropped her arms and turned back to the table she'd been clearing. "Besides that, I don't need any help."

She was lying, and they both knew it.

"Are you doing all this on your own?" He already knew the answer. Levi crossed the room so he was on the other side of the table from her and she couldn't avoid looking at him. He followed her lead and started to gather up the dirty glassware the way she was.

"I am." She threw him a look. "And I'm doing just fine." She abandoned the glasses and started to snatch up napkins.

"I didn't mean to imply that you weren't doing fine." He followed her to the next table. Maybe showing up at her place the way he had was a bad idea. Maybe he should have just stayed away.

But he couldn't have done that. Not for anything. The last ten years had been hard enough, and that's when there'd been actual physical distance between them. Just being back in town, knowing he was only a few minutes away, had been torture for the less than twenty-four hours he'd been back. The pull to her had been magnetic. Even if there hadn't been a stupid help wanted ad, there was no doubt in his mind that Levi would have found a reason to get over to Ever After Ranch. And now that he was here...not touching her, not pulling her into his arms...it was hard. *Very* hard.

"Good." She shot him a look over her shoulder.

Yes. She'd definitely developed a bit of an edge since he'd been gone. He liked it.

"Because I'm doing more than fine," she said.

Levi didn't think it was worth mentioning the exhaustion that was threaded through her voice, or the ever so slight circles under her beautiful blue eyes. She was tired. And maybe she was doing fine. More than fine even. But she needed help. Even if only so she could take a rest. That much was certain.

"I got that." He grinned. "But you did put the ad on Facebook, didn't you?"

She dropped her head and shook it before looking up at him with a bashful smile. "I'm afraid to admit that I did that in a moment of weakness late last night."

"It's not weakness to need help, Hope."

"I've never needed it before. And I don't need it now. I was just tired and it was late and—"

"Give me the job."

She put a hand on her hip. "I told you, Levi. I don't *need* help. I'm not hiring."

"Your ad says differently."

"I didn't think you were even on Facebook."

Aw! So she was looking!

He tried and failed to hide his smile. "I'm not. Logan is."

"Of course."

She shook her head and turned back to her work.

"So you'll hire me?" He was relentless. He needed to be. Because now that he was there, looking at her, talking to her, just *being* with her, he needed more. *Much* more. Even if that was only in the shape of working for her. He'd take what he could get. Because dammit, he'd missed her. "I can do whatever you need." He moved swiftly around the table and grabbed the tray full of dirty glasses. He lifted it easily and turned to put it...*where?* She pointed to a cart and covered her face with her hand.

"I don't really need anyone to do dishes."

"But you do need someone?" Levi deposited the tray on the cart and immediately started stacking chairs. "I can get these for you."

"You need to take the covers off first." She shook her head, but he saw the smile on her face.

"Done." With a flourish, he started to whip off chair covers and throw them in a pile. "See? I'm very helpful."

"I don't know about that." Hope laughed. It was a sound that filled every cell in his body and froze him in place. Careful to keep his face as neutral as he possibly could, he looked at her and waited for her to say more. "Are you handy? Like with building things? I have a few projects..." She trailed off. "I'm going to regret this."

"You're not!" But she might, because as much as he knew he *needed* to spend time with her, a part of him—a very deep part—started to regret his impulsive decision to take the job. Could he really handle being around Hope Turner again? Could he handle being so close to her without *being* with her? He had no idea. "It'll be great," he said. But he couldn't be sure who he was reassuring. "I'm very handy. I can build all kinds of things. Between my work years ago on the ranch and various odd jobs I did on the boat, I have mad skills."

"Mad skills, huh?"

He nodded and winked. "Definitely."

She looked at her feet and shook her head as if she were trying to talk herself out of what they both knew she was going to say. "Okay," she said when she looked up again. "I'll hire you. But only because I need a few things done around here. Minimum wage. And it's a trial basis only."

"Deal." He stepped quickly to cross the room and held out a hand.

Hope placed her hand in his and the heat of her skin shot through him, directly to his heart. He knew she felt it too because she looked him straight in the eye and said, "I still don't know about this."

Neither did he. Because now that he was back in Hope's life, even in this capacity, he wasn't sure he could ever leave again.

Chapter Three

SPRING WAS Hope's favorite time in Glacier Falls, the town that got its name from the spectacular display of crashing ice-cold water of the Jumbo Creek that came directly off the Jumbo Glacier that sat high in the mountains. The falls were situated almost at the center of town, with a natural park serving as the town square and popular gathering place for the townspeople. The river was flowing fast, with the spring thaw, and Hope knew the falls would be particularly spectacular now. She made a mental note to swing past them on her way home.

The trees were just starting to leaf out, filling the streets with that fresh green that made everything seem new and hopeful. Over the last few years as tourism had grown, the town had started to do a really beautiful job of planting flowers along Main Street and the shop owners took up the challenge as well, trying to outdo one another with their own displays. The overall effect was absolutely gorgeous and Hope always had the distinct impression that she was walking through a Hallmark movie. It was no wonder more and more brides were choosing her town as the perfect venue to tie the knot. Of course, the fact that it was only a few hours out of the big city helped.

But Hope couldn't help but take some of the credit, too. The creation of Ever After Ranch had been huge in drawing more brides away from the city and into the mountains for their nuptials. It was a fact that she was very proud of. She'd gotten busy. *Too* busy, maybe. She currently had a two-year waiting list for an available summer wedding date. She hadn't really ventured too far into the winter wedding business, but it was something she'd consider if she wasn't so bloody tired.

Or if she had help.

You have help now.

The little voice in her head piped up, reminding her that she did indeed have help—whether she liked it or not—in the form of Levi Langdon. And the jury was still out on whether she liked it or not. Seeing him again had been...shocking.

And also pretty damn nice.

She knew she should be angry or hurt or any combination of those things toward him. It wasn't his fault they hadn't worked out all those years ago. Not really. He'd done the right thing, breaking up with her. He couldn't stay and she wouldn't leave and they both knew it. A relationship couldn't survive terms like that. It was the only choice for the younger versions of themselves. No matter how much they'd loved each other.

But that was then.

Hope shook her head to clear the voice that was definitely starting to push its limits with her patience and pulled open the door to the Glacier Falls medical clinic and Doctor Friesen's office. She didn't really have time to take off in the middle of the day for a doctor appointment, but her exhaustion was getting harder and harder to ignore. And despite her uncertainty about hiring Levi, he was actually working hard and in the few days he'd been working for her, he'd actually proved himself to be quite useful.

It was too bad she was going to have to let him go.

He may be a good worker, and she may completely understand why they had to break up all those years ago but that didn't make it any easier for him to be around. Whatever attracted them together when they were kids hadn't lessened over the years. Quite the opposite, really. Having Levi in such close proximity was torture. Especially because there was no way she could risk falling for him again.

"Good morning, Hope." Sarah, Doctor Friesen's nurse and receptionist, who also happened to be one of Hope's oldest friends, greeted her with her usual smile. "It's a gorgeous day out there, isn't it? I tell you what, if I wasn't working for a doctor, I'd be tempted to call in sick and play hooky." She leaned across the desk as if she were telling Hope a big secret, but then burst into a great big booming laugh. It was well known all over town that both Sarah and Doctor Friesen had maybe less than five sick days combined since they'd started working together almost five years ago. Not only were they incredibly hardworking, but they both somehow seemed completely immune to the illnesses that constantly passed through the clinic doors. Which was a good thing because Sarah was a single mom to a very busy six-year-old girl. The woman definitely didn't have time to be sick.

"It really is beautiful out there." Hope replied with a smile of her own when Sarah's laughter died down. "I hope you get to enjoy it later."

"You know I will." Sarah winked dramatically. "Rory has her first soccer practice later, and there's nothing I like more than standing on the sidelines, cheering."

Hope had no doubt that was completely true. She'd never met a more devoted mother than Sarah.

"Please tell me you're not coaching?" Hope wouldn't be surprised if the answer was yes, because Sarah seemed determined to be both mother and father to her little girl ever since her husband passed away suddenly when Rory was just a baby. Hope couldn't help but worry about her friend at times, although she seemed happy enough with her life. Sarah worked so hard for everyone else; it would be nice to see her friend take a little time for herself.

"No way." Sarah held up her hands. "I have my limits," she said. "And anything physical is definitely it. I'm a fabulous team mom, but there is no way I could get this body to run around a field."

"I'm sure you'd have no trouble keeping up."

Sarah laughed again. "I appreciate it, but the last time I had any time for any physical activity, well…I can't remember when that time was. And all these extra pounds are definitely not compatible with soccer."

Hope shook her head and wanted to tell her friend she was being ridiculous. It wasn't the first time Sarah had made negative comments about her body, and nothing she could say while standing in the doctor's office was likely to make a difference, but she made a mental note to try to get together for a proper catch up soon.

"Besides, Brody Morris volunteered to coach the kids," Sarah continued. "Isn't that nice of him? I mean, he doesn't even have kids. The man should get a medal. He's so great with them."

"Brody's a great guy," Hope agreed. He was also the chef and owner of the local restaurant Birchwood, and the two of them had worked together on more than one occasion for catering. "He's pretty hot, too, don't you think?"

Sarah's face turned bright red, but her wide smile vanished at the same time. "I hadn't noticed." She shook her head and looked down. "You can go into room four, Hope. Doctor Friesen shouldn't be too long."

Hope hesitated, unsure of what more she should say, having clearly hit on a sensitive topic. "Thanks," she finally muttered. "And let me know when Rory has her first game. I'd love to come cheer her on with you. And maybe we can catch up a little."

The smile returned to her friend's face as she looked up. "I'd like that, Hope. Thanks."

A few moments later, Hope found herself perched on the edge of the examination bed, the thin paper crinkling loudly beneath her, just the way she had been since she was a kid and Doctor Friesen had taken over for his predecessor, whom she could never remember. She took in all the posters on the walls that advertised various medications, including one for birth control. She almost laughed out loud. It had been a *very* long time since that had been a consideration.

But it might not be that way for long.

The thought popped into her head so unexpectedly it actually caused her to blush. Just because Levi was back in town didn't mean that anything was going to happen between them. And the fact that she'd entertained it, even for a second, was more than a little disturbing.

Was it?

A knock on the door followed by the doctor's arrival saved Hope from herself and her thoughts that were rapidly taking a turn. "Hi, Hope. It's good to see you." The doctor made his way into the room, and sat on his stool before turning and giving her his familiar friendly smile. She swung her feet, feeling like a child.

"It's nice to see you, too."

"But not that nice, or you wouldn't be here today, would you?" He transitioned smoothly into doctor mode. "What brings you in today? Your chart says you're tired."

It sounded even more ridiculous when it came from the doctor's mouth. She was wasting everyone's time. Hope shook her head, but then nodded with a shrug. "I am. I know it sounds really stupid and—"

"Not at all." His kindly face didn't reflect any annoyance at all, only concern. "In fact, I think it's very important to listen to your body and if you're not feeling right, like something is off, you shouldn't ignore it. Now, tell me, what exactly is going on with you?"

Despite her initial urge to turn around and leave, Hope was put at ease the way she always was with Doctor Friesen. It must be a skill they teach at medical school, how to get patients talking. For the next few minutes, she relayed all of her symptoms, which consisted mostly of complete and utter exhaustion no matter how much sleep she was getting and some occasional pain in her abdomen.

"This pain." Doctor Friesen stopped her. "Can you describe it?"

Hope shrugged. "Kind of like a menstrual cramp, I guess. But different. More pressure." She shook her head. "I don't know, it's hard to explain. I actually thought it might be period related, but…"

The doctor tilted his head. "And how have your periods been? Normal?"

She hadn't stopped to think about it until he asked, but she'd always been regular with her cycle, and it had been a little *off* lately. "Heavier," she told the doctor.

He made a note in his chart. He still used paper charts, a fact that she knew drove Sarah crazy, because she'd been trying —and failing—to move him to a computerized system. Hope stifled her smile as he continued to ask her questions. "And how is your appetite? You look like you might have lost a little weight from the last time I saw you."

She shrugged. She hadn't given her appetite any thought. She was eating. Mostly. "I guess I'm not actually that hungry these days."

He nodded and continued to make notes for a few minutes before putting down his pen and spinning on his stool to face her. "Okay. I'm going to listen to your heart, look in your throat, and all that stuff, but we're also going to send you for a blood workup, and my chart shows you're due for a physical, so we should probably take care of that, too."

Hope sighed.

"I know, no one likes to visit the doctor, but not to worry, Hope. We'll figure it out. It's not normal for an otherwise healthy young woman like yourself to not feel one hundred percent." He pulled out his stethoscope and pressed it to her chest. "I hear that you have help around the ranch finally."

She shook her head and rolled her eyes. "News travels fast around here."

He winked. "You're not surprised, I hope? Besides, I think it's a good thing. Especially while you're not feeling on top of your game. A little help around there is exactly what the doctor ordered." He looked her in the eye. "At least until we figure out what's going on with you, okay? It's never a good idea to wear yourself down."

She nodded, because there didn't seem to be much of a choice. Doctor Friesen always did have a way of taking her right back to her youth. She followed his orders when she was a child; she wasn't about to stop now.

Levi could stay.

For now.

"I know I keep saying it every day, but I still can't believe you're here."

Levi kissed his auntie on the forehead as she handed him a cup of coffee and he took a seat at the kitchen table. *His* seat. Or at least the one that used to be his when he was a kid. Old habits die hard.

"I know." Of course he knew; she'd been telling him as much on repeat for the last few days. Not that he minded. Levi blew on the coffee before setting it down. "It really is good to be back."

"Is it?" Aunt Debbie never did beat around the bush. She took her seat across from him and gazed steadily at him until he smiled and nodded.

"It is." It was an honest answer. "I missed you." Another honest answer.

"But you didn't miss everything."

He shook his head. "No. But that doesn't matter now." He waited for her to challenge him, but she simply smiled a sad smile and sat back.

"No," she said. "It doesn't. I'm just really glad you're here. I've missed you so much, Levi."

"She has, it's true." A familiar voice behind him had Levi jumping up and out of his seat to give his cousin a bear hug.

Levi pulled Katie into a tight hug and lifted her the way he had when they were kids. "Finally," he said when he put her down. "Where have you been? I've been waiting to see you for days."

She laughed and attempted to smooth her dark ponytail back off her face. "I've been here and there," she said with a wink before moving across the floor to help herself to a coffee. "I'm a busy girl."

Levi shook his head when Aunt Deb rolled her eyes. "Too busy to help your brother and me around here, that's for sure."

"Hey." Katie pretended to look offended. "I'm taking a very demanding course. When I graduate, I'll be able to take this ranch to the next level."

"Whatever that is."

"You wait and see, Mom. I have ideas." She turned to look at Levi, her face a mask of seriousness. "Do you know how much potential there is in expansion and diversification?" Katie had been taking a business degree online in recent months and even though Logan had warned him that she was full of ideas for how to improve operations around the ranch, Levi hadn't expected his once completely indifferent cousin to be so passionate about it.

"I guess I never really thought about it."

Katie put her hands on the table and leaned over as she spoke, clearly excited to share with someone. "There are lots of options, you know, Levi? It doesn't have to always be the way we've done things. I mean, look at Hope Turner. She's completely changed everything about her ranch and she's killing it."

She *was* killing it. At least, that was as much as he could deduce from only working for her for a few days. She had a well-run organization and looking at her calendar, she was booked up for almost every spring and summer weekend for the next few years. It was impressive what she'd done. And all on her own.

But that was changing now, too. She didn't have to do it all on her own. He was back and more than happy to help. If she wanted him to, that was.

Sure, she'd hired him, but Levi couldn't help but feel that he was going to get fired soon. Almost from the moment she'd agreed to let him help out, Hope hadn't been able to make eye contact with him. He knew Hope. Having him around couldn't be easy.

Just the way it wasn't easy to be so close to her and not be able to have her.

It was torture. But a torture he'd happily continue to put himself through. After all, it was Hope. He'd do anything for her.

"Hope's place is pretty incredible," he said as soon as Katie let him get in a word. "I'm super impressed with what she's doing around there."

"It must be nice to be spending time with Hope again, Levi." The question was innocent enough, but as Levi looked across the table to his aunt, she wore a wicked grin on her face, one that she tried—and failed—to cover by taking a sip of her coffee.

"It is," he answered honestly. "But, she is my boss." He took a deep gulp of the hot coffee and put his mug down hard on the table. "And even though she told me not to come in until after lunch, I wanted to stop by the hardware store and grab some supplies before heading over there."

"You always were a hard worker."

"Sounds like someone is trying to suck up."

Levi looked in turn at the women at the table. Aunt Deb looked almost the same as she always had. There was a little more gray streaked in her long, thick braid that hung down her back, but the adoring smile she always had for him was exactly the same.

Katie, on the other hand, had changed. Somewhere along the line, she'd grown up from the precocious bratty little sister she'd always been, to a feisty, sassy woman with ideas way too big for this town.

He shook his head and laughed. "It's good to be home. I'll see you both later."

It wasn't until he was in his truck driving out of the yard that Levi realized he'd referred to the ranch as *home*.

His trip to Glacier Falls was only supposed to be temporary. Sticking around had never been part of the plan.

But plans could change.

Chapter Four

BY THE TIME Hope had her blood drawn and got back from town, she was ready for a nap. That is, if there were time for a nap. Which there most certainly was not.

She pulled up next to Levi's truck at the barn and dammit if her stomach didn't do a little flip just knowing he was inside working.

For her.

Well, not really *for her.* But still...

Maybe she shouldn't let him go.

Maybe the physical ache he caused every time he was close to her was the price to pay to have some help around the ranch. Hope sighed and pulled herself out of her truck. She really did need to get things ready for the wedding this weekend. And Levi was a good worker...

Dammit.

Her mind was clearly already made up. Besides, Doctor Friesen had told her to try to rest as much as possible. At least until they figured out what was wrong with her. He seemed confident that it was nothing more than a vitamin deficiency, but still. There was no point running herself into the ground while they waited to figure out what it was.

With another sigh, Hope made her way inside the barn and immediately stopped short.

"What the hell?"

The space that had been largely empty and swept clean only a few days ago had been completely reset with furniture. After each event, Hope had a habit of moving all the tables and restacking all the chairs so she could properly clean the floors and get ready for the next event—which she'd done on Monday morning. It was a monumental amount of work to move each table back into place, but it was the only way to make sure the space was properly cleaned—which was why she made it a priority. It was that kind of attention to detail that made her the best.

More than normal, Hope hadn't been looking forward to getting reset for the next wedding. She shook her head and looked around, not quite sure to trust what she was seeing.

Maybe she was having hallucinations, too?

Hope rubbed her eyes and then laughed at herself. She wasn't dreaming.

She was wide awake.

Slowly, she stepped inside and took inventory of what had been set up.

Ten tables.

Each with ten chairs.

A rectangular head table with seating for eight.

She didn't even have to look at her book to know that was the right number of tables and chairs.

Hope circled the room, mentally measuring the distance between each table.

Perfectly spaced.

Everything looked exactly like the diagram she had in her master binder. Even though she knew exactly what she was doing, and had done almost every table configuration dozens of times, she still never left anything to chance. Perfection was in the details. She moved a chair slightly to the left and shook her head in wonder.

"Is it okay?"

Levi's voice jarred her and she jumped a little before turning around to face him.

"Sorry," he said. "I didn't mean to scare you."

"You…it's okay." What was the point in denying it? She'd always been easy to scare. Hope shook her head and looked around again. "Did you…" She turned back to him. "Did you do all this?"

He nodded and Hope tried in vain not to notice the way his eyes crinkled when he smiled. *Dammit. Why did he have to be so bloody good-looking?*

"I did. I found the diagram in your binder and when I was done with the floor, I thought—"

"The floor? I swept it on Monday."

Levi actually looked bashful as he shrugged. Annoyingly, it was cute. "I thought you might like it polished."

"Polished?" Hope swallowed hard before taking a closer look at the floor. Damned if it wasn't extra shiny and *polished*. "You polished the floor? This morning?"

He nodded. "It was on a list at the back of your binder."

She knew exactly what list he was talking about. It was her master list of things she'd like to get done, but that would probably have to wait until the end of the busy season. But he'd done it. He'd taken something off the list.

Dammit. She really couldn't fire him now.

"I hope it's okay. I wasn't trying to step on your toes or anything, but you make it really easy to get things done with your lists. I mean, you've always been organized, but…" He shook his head in admiration. "Damn, you've taken it to the next level."

She couldn't help it. As much as she didn't want Levi to get to her, he did. Just the way he always had. With a smile and a wink and basically any words coming out of his mouth in that smooth-like-caramel voice of his, and she was a goner.

"I don't know about that." Hope looked at her feet before Levi could see her blush at the compliment.

"But it's okay?" he asked again. "I know you like things a certain way, and I was just trying to help so the last thing I would want to do is make more work for you."

Hope looked up into his eyes and saw nothing there but genuine care. She didn't even look at the tables and chairs again before she nodded. "It's perfect, Levi. Thank you. Really. The idea of setting this up today was exhausting me just by thinking about it. You've really saved me a lot of work."

His grin split his face. He looked like a proud schoolboy receiving praise from his favorite teacher. "Good. That's my job, right? To help you?"

Hope sighed. *Definitely no way she could let him go now.* She was just going to have to live with the butterflies that had taken up residence in her stomach ever since he showed up. "I guess it is."

"That's right, it is." Levi reached out his hand to her. "Come on, I want to show you something."

She eyed him and his outstretched hand. Having him in close proximity was one thing. *Touching him* was something completely different. She tucked her hands into her back pocket. "What's that?"

If Levi was offended, or even noticed that she hadn't taken his hand, he didn't show it. Instead, his smile only got bigger as he said, "Just wait until you see it."

Levi couldn't help it. Seeing Hope happy—especially when it was because of him—gave him a thrill. An even bigger thrill than reeling in a major catch on his favorite fishing boat. Way bigger.

"Seriously," he said when she still hadn't moved. He retracted his proffered hand. Maybe he shouldn't be so bold with her, she was obviously struggling with it, but he couldn't help it. It was just so easy to be with her. Maybe too easy. But it did feel like old times. He needed to remember that it wasn't. Far from it. "Come on," he urged. "I promise you'll like it more than having this room set up."

She laughed, but started walking with him. "I don't know about that. This is pretty fantastic. Now instead of dragging furniture around, I can take a little more time doing the place settings. Or maybe having a nap."

Hope added the last bit so softly, he wasn't sure she'd said it. Levi snuck a glance at her pretty face. She did look tired. She likely could use a nap. And if he made it possible for her to do so, well, that was only a good thing.

They walked across the barn to the back sliding doors, where Levi's surprise lay just beyond. But right before he opened the door to reveal what he'd been working on, he had a flash of inspiration. He spun around so quickly he almost bumped into her, but Hope took a quick step backward, putting space between them. "Let's make a deal." He forced himself to ignore the heat that flashed through his body at her nearness.

"A deal?"

Levi nodded. "Exactly." He couldn't help but smile. "I've already saved you hours of work, right?"

She narrowed her eyes suspiciously, but nodded in agreement. "You did."

"That's right, I did." He laughed at himself, and once again focused. "Okay, so the deal is…since I've already made your day better…" She shook her head and rolled her eyes, but

Levi just laughed and continued, "If you like what I'm about to show you, you go out with me tonight."

Her face instantly paled and she shook her head. "I don't think—"

"Not like, out-out." He held up his hands in a weak effort to keep her from running away. "I mean like out with friends, out. Logan, Katie, and I were going to go into town tonight for Musical Bingo at the Knot."

"Musical Bingo?"

"You've heard of it?"

She shook her head.

"How is that?" He pretended to look shocked. "I'm told it's the place to be on Wednesday nights. Apparently there's some killer drink specials, too."

"I don't get out much."

"Then we should change that."

She tilted her head and eyed him suspiciously.

"I'm not saying a date," he reassured her, despite the fact that a date was exactly what he wanted. The impact of that thought hit him square in the gut. Dammit. He *did* want a date. Hell, he wanted a whole lot more when it came to Hope. It had only been a few days since he'd been back in town, but he didn't need any longer to know what he had never forgotten.

He loved Hope Turner.

Levi swallowed hard. Something told him that declaring that love for her at that precise moment would not have the desired effect. He smiled his biggest, most charming smile. "I'm just saying it would be a fun night out with friends. Katie and Logan assure me that it's hilarious and full of all the classic sing-alongs from our youth."

"I don't know." She shook her head and started to back away, but he stopped her.

"Hey, you haven't seen my surprise yet."

Levi was well aware that he'd already put a bit of a stipulation on the surprise he wanted to show her and that probably wasn't fair, but screw it. He didn't want to be fair. Not if it meant having a chance to get Hope away from the ranch and see her having a bit of fun that didn't include work. He may not have been back in town long, but it wasn't hard to see that she needed a break and she was definitely long overdue for having some fun.

She sighed, obviously torn between wanting to see what he was hiding and getting out of the possibility of going out to Musical Bingo. "Okay, fine," she said, surprising them both.

"Fine?"

She nodded. "Fine. It's a deal. If I like whatever it is you're hiding out there, I'll go to bingo. But not before I have a nap."

"Deal." He wasn't about to argue those terms. Before she could change her mind, he spun around and with a big push, shoved the barn door to the side to reveal what he'd been working on.

Levi didn't even have to turn around to know she liked it. A lot.

Behind him, Hope gasped. A moment later, she walked past him, toward the surprise, and held her hand out.

The other day, he'd been flipping through her master binder. Of course, he'd been impressed with her organization, but that was nothing new. Hope always was super organized with things. But more than that, he'd been impressed with the lists he'd found at the back. Pages filled with her plans to improve things and added features that she could offer couples. One of those things had been the arch he'd been working on. The arch she was currently speechless over.

"How did you…it's…you did this?" She ran her hand down the smooth wood and walked through it as she examined every inch of it. "Levi, it's…wow." Finally, Hope turned to look at him. "My binder," she said with a nod. "You looked at my lists."

"I did." He nodded and crossed his arms over his chest to keep from reaching out to her. "I hope that's okay. I just really wanted to make sure you didn't regret your decision to hire me on and...well, I really want to help, Hope."

For a moment, she looked as if she might cry. "I see that." She blinked hard and laughed, the emotional moment gone. "Okay, you win. What time do we leave?"

"Ohh, ohh, that's 'Wild Thing'!" Hope raised her dauber marker in the air for a moment before quickly pressing it down on the appropriate square.

Across the table, Katie waved her arms in the air and sang along with the song. It only took a moment before Hope joined her with the chorus.

They broke out in laughter and Hope reached for her beer. As she lifted it to her lips, she met Levi's eyes. He watched her with a grin on his face, so Hope winked and took a sip of her beer.

She had to admit, she was having a good time. Musical Bingo turned out to be a blast and was without a doubt the most fun she'd had at a bar in years.

Not that she spent much time in bars. And not that the Knot was really a traditional bar. It was Glacier Fall's only pub and one of the only places to eat. Hope had been there plenty of times, but she couldn't honestly remember the last time she'd been there later than the dinner hour.

She'd been missing out.

"Having a good time?" Levi asked unnecessarily, right as the song changed.

Hope and Katie both leaned into the song, listening intently before they cried out at the same time, "Walk of Life!" And then dissolved into giggles as they each daubed the appropriate squares on the cards in front of them.

"This is awesome," Hope said when they were done marking their squares. "I don't know why I didn't know about this."

"Because you work all the time." Katie laughed. "But now that you know…"

"I'll totally come again. And maybe I can even get Sarah to get a babysitter."

"Sarah Lewis?" It was Levi who asked. "I haven't seen her in ages. How's she doing?"

Hope shrugged. "Good, I guess. She married Josh Lewis. Remember him?"

"Of course."

"And you heard the news then?" Katie jumped in. "It was so sad when he died. Their little girl was just a baby and they were on holidays at the lake."

"The lake? Cedar Springs?"

Hope nodded. Cedar Springs was the popular resort community less than an hour away from them in the mountains. The lake was a popular place for all of them to hang out when they were younger. And it had a lot of good memories. For most of them.

"It was really tragic." Hope took over the story. "They were on the beach and Josh noticed a child in distress out by the raft." She swallowed hard. "So he jumped in. Didn't even hesitate."

"That's terrible," Levi said, obviously figuring out how the story would end.

"He saved the boy," Katie said. "But he didn't come up again. And with all the chaos, by the time anyone got to him, it was too late."

Levi looked between them all as he absorbed the story. "That's absolutely awful."

Hope nodded. "It is, but it was years ago now, and Sarah's doing really well. She started working with Doctor Friesen right before it happened, and she has a lot of family support in town for her little girl, Rory. She's really the best mom. She seems really happy now."

"Well, that's good to hear."

"Speaking of hearing…" Katie pointed up into the air as a new song started to play.

"Walking on Sunshine!" Hope and Katie called out together and immediately the mood was lighter.

"Logan." Katie elbowed her brother. "You aren't playing."

"Sure I am." He lifted his mug of beer, not looking at her, but instead at something, or more likely, someone—like the beautiful brunette—across the room.

"No," Katie insisted. "You're not. Look, you've missed the last three songs."

"Here." He shoved his card toward his sister, put down his mug and pushed up from the table. "You take care of this for me. I have something I need to do."

"Logan! Come on. That's no fun."

Logan turned around and grinned at his sister. "Oh, I think it will be plenty of fun."

Katie rolled her eyes and looked at Levi. "Nothing's changed."

Hope didn't know about that, but she didn't bother saying so. There was a time when Logan was definitely more interested in her twin sister than any other woman in town. Not that he'd admit it back then. And there was probably even less of a chance she'd get him to admit it now.

Hope shook her head in Logan's direction and caught Levi's eye as she turned back to her bingo cards.

"Maybe things could have been different."

She froze, totally caught off guard. *Of course* things could have been different. But he'd—

"If only Faith had even the slightest idea that he'd been in to her."

45

Oh. He wasn't talking about them. Hope picked up her bottle of beer in an attempt to hide her embarrassment. Maybe it was her exhaustion, or the little bit of beer she had....maybe it was just sitting close to Levi and feeling both so familiar and also totally strange with him. It could have been any number of things that had made her assume he was talking about her.

As if he read her thoughts, he put his hand on hers, just for a moment, long enough to send a shot of desire racing straight through her, and said, "A lot of things could have been different."

Hope opened her mouth and shut it again, only vaguely aware that she likely resembled a guppy.

"You're the One That I Want!" Katie yelled across the table as the song changed.

Happy for the distraction, Hope raised her dauber and studied her bingo card. It took her a moment to recover from the awkward moment. Was Levi really saying what she thought he'd been saying?

A lot of things could have been different.

Of course they could have! But he'd left.

Or maybe she was reading way more into it than there was. That was probably the case. He was just talking about Logan and Faith. A couple that never was. She turned her head and watched Logan at the bar trying to chat up the brunette she didn't recognize.

The idea of Faith and Logan together actually made her laugh out loud. Her sister held nothing but disdain for Logan Langdon. Everything about him seemed to irritate her, and he'd always had so much fun pushing her buttons. Which was exactly why years ago Hope and Levi had decided that Logan teased Faith so badly because he secretly liked her. It was a theory. And one they'd been pretty sold on, despite Logan's denials.

"Hey." Levi nudged her elbow, pulling her from her

thoughts. He reached across her and pointed at her bingo card. "You have a line. You have a bingo."

Hope followed to where he was pointing and sure enough, she did. "Bingo!" She grabbed her card, raised it in the air, and laughed herself out of the chair.

"You have to go up there." Katie pointed to the DJ booth. "Take your card up and you'll win a prize."

Hope didn't hesitate. She loved prizes. Not that she ever won them. Besides, a little space from Levi and the memories that relentlessly popped into her head could only be a good thing.

It had been a good night. A really good night.

Levi couldn't remember the last time he'd laughed so hard. After Hope won the first round, they'd continued to play for three more. Even Logan, shot down by the brunette at the bar, rejoined them for the last two rounds.

It had felt good to hang out with his cousins again. And Hope.

It felt *really* good to hang out with Hope.

Like old times.

He couldn't let himself go there. Not yet. Even though he *really* wanted to. More than anything, did he ever want to go there.

"That was good," he said to Hope, who had been quiet ever since they'd gotten in the truck. He'd insisted on picking her up earlier to make sure she didn't bail out at the last minute, and of course, any excuse to spend extra time with her, he was going to take it. "Are you glad you came?"

"I am." She yawned deeply. "But I'm so tired. I don't know how I'm going to get anything done tomorrow."

"Don't worry about it." He moved to reach across the bench seat of his truck to grab her hand, but caught himself and placed it firmly back on the steering wheel. "That's why you hired me, right?" He grinned in her direction, but she wasn't looking. Her eyes were closed, and her head dipped.

She was asleep.

Levi didn't bother stifling his smile. She'd always been so cute when she fell asleep in his truck. Of course, that's when they'd been kids. Maybe he shouldn't have kept her up so late? He felt a flicker of guilt. After all, she had already said that she was pretty tired.

Well, he'd let her sleep then.

Levi focused on the mountain roads in front of him, keeping a special eye out for any deer lingering in the ditches. They had a tendency to jump out at the most random times. The drive back to Ever After Ranch from town was only about fifteen minutes, but Hope slept through the entire thing. Levi had been hoping that he might get invited in for a nightcap, or might even be able to sneak a little kiss on the cheek. He wasn't looking for much. Well, he was, but he'd be patient. After all, he was the one who'd screwed up the best thing he'd ever had. If it took some time for him to convince her that he still cared, he'd take that time.

"We're here." Levi spoke softly, almost unwilling to wake her after he pulled up in the yard in front of the house. Her head leaned against the window and she looked so peaceful, he really did hate to wake her. But she couldn't spend the night in the truck. He tried again, this time shaking her leg softly. "Hope? We're home."

She groaned a little, but made no move to wake up.

There was no help for it.

Levi slipped from the truck and went around to her door. He opened it slowly, careful not to jar her. He leaned in and unbuckled her before pulling her gently into his arms. She groaned and nuzzled her head against his chest.

Holding her was quite possibly the very best feeling in the

world. Levi took in a deep breath and held her closer before turning toward the house.

Hope never used to lock the door, and he hoped that hadn't changed. He shifted her in his arms and tried the door handle.

Locked.

Dammit.

He really didn't want to have to put her down. Not for anything. But as willing as he was to do it, he couldn't stand on the porch with her all night. He glanced around, his eyes landing on the ledge above the door.

It was worth a shot.

Levi stretched as far as he could without dropping her and reached for what he hoped would be a key. Sure enough, his fingers wrapped around metal.

A moment later, the key was in the lock and he was inside.

It had been years since he'd been in the Turner house. But he remembered it as if it were his own. He'd spent so much time there, preferring Hope's family to his uncle's company more often than not. And Mr. and Mrs. Turner had been so warm and welcoming to him. No doubt they'd thought he would end up their son-in-law one day.

He couldn't help but wonder what they'd thought of him after he broke Hope's heart.

A stab of guilt hit him in the chest.

He'd never be able to apologize to them for hurting their daughter. They'd died four years ago. Logan called to tell him. It was the only other time Levi had been tempted to return to town. To be there for Hope.

But she likely wouldn't have wanted him. Not then, when her heart was already fractured into a million pieces. He only would have made it worse. And the very last thing Levi wanted to do was cause Hope any more pain.

He looked down at her face, even more beautiful in sleep.

No. He'd never hurt her. Not again.

Levi made his way up the stairs and hesitated at the top, unsure whether she was still in her childhood bedroom. The one he'd snuck into more times than he could count. Second door on the left. He remembered it well. But ultimately he turned right, toward the master suite. Hope would have moved into her parents' old room.

Sure enough, the moment he walked through the door, he knew it was Hope's space. Soft and simple. The bed was made with an oversized white duvet and pale-blue throw pillows. Carefully, he pulled the covers back and laid Hope down on her sheets.

He slipped her boots from her feet, but that's as far as he went. She'd be mortified to find that he'd undressed her, even if it would be more comfortable.

And he'd seen her naked hundreds of times before.

That was a detail he definitely didn't need to be reminded of. Not ever.

Staying strong against temptation, Levi pulled the blankets up over her and kissed her on the forehead. "Good night, beautiful." He brushed a strand of hair from her cheek and forced himself to slip from the room despite the fact that every cell in his body demanded to stay.

Chapter Five

THE NEXT MORNING, Hope woke feeling as if she'd been on an all-night bender. Her head ached, her stomach cramped and clenched, and inexplicably, she was still wearing her clothes from the night before. She hadn't been drunk. Not from one beer. She'd cut herself off after only one because she'd been so tired, she didn't want the beer to make her even more drowsy.

She rubbed at her head and that's when she remembered.

A kiss.

On her forehead.

Levi had kissed her on the forehead.

But when?

How was it that she had no memory of Levi kissing her? It didn't make any sense. Was it at the bar? Or...*no!*

She flipped over so quickly, the pain in her stomach almost made her vomit. But she needed to know. *Was he in the bed with her?*

No. The bed was empty. *Of course it was.*

She would never have let him spend the night. Hell, she hadn't even kissed him yet.

Except he had kissed her.

She touched her fingers to her forehead again.

Hadn't he?

Hope groaned and rolled over. Her feelings were all too confusing. And there *were* feelings.

There was no denying that. The feelings were all there. And they were all real. Heck, they'd probably never left. She wasn't sure exactly what they were, but she was definitely having feelings for Levi. *Major* ones.

Not that lying there still wearing her clothes from the night before was going to sort any of that out.

That was a whole different problem, in fact. Never in her life, even when she was young and made her share of poor decisions, had she ever had no recollection of how she'd ended up in bed the night before. That was definitely not normal.

Slowly, Hope pulled herself out of bed and made her way to the bathroom. The cramps in her abdomen intensified when she stood up, but she managed to make it into the bathroom, start the shower, and swallow down a few painkillers. The heat of the water helped, or maybe it was the painkillers, but by the time she finished in the shower, she felt much better and the idea of facing her day, even though she was already getting a way later start than she would have liked, was finally bearable.

Hope wasn't surprised to see Levi's truck outside the barn when she pulled up in her golf cart. The sight of it made her smile. For as much as she had her doubts, hiring Levi had turned out to be a really good decision. Besides the fact that he worked harder than she would have thought, he went way over and above what she'd expected, and maybe most importantly, she really enjoyed his company. More than she cared to admit.

"Good morning," Levi called the moment she walked into the barn. He was across the room, pulling linens from one of her bins. She watched for a moment while he expertly shook out the tablecloth and laid it out over the table before picking up the steamer.

She shook her head with a grin and made her way across to him. "Where did you learn to do that?"

He held up the steamer and gave her a campy grin before getting back to work. "I have skills you don't even know about."

She couldn't help but laugh. "Clearly."

She watched for a few more moments before he asked, "Am I doing okay?" He paused before steaming out a wrinkle. "Because if you want to jump in and take over, I won't be offended."

Normally, Hope would have done just that. But she shook her head and pulled out a chair. "You're doing a great job. I'm happy to sit and watch."

"You could help, ya know?" He teased. "After all, I am just the help. You're the brains behind this."

She knew she probably should, but she was just so damn tired. Guilt flooded through her. Not once since she'd started Ever After Ranch had she sat back and let anyone else do the preparation for a wedding. Not ever. She took her events incredibly seriously. After all, the happy couples were putting the most important day of their lives into her hands. It was the least she could do.

But on that particular morning, Hope had put all her energy into just getting herself into the barn. It didn't seem like a bad idea at all to let Levi set the tables. She propped her head up with one arm. "No." She stifled a yawn. "I think I'll let you handle it today."

Levi eyed her suspiciously. He looked as if he wanted to say something, but he closed his mouth and looked away. His silence only lasted a moment, however. "Are you okay? You look..."

"What? I look what?"

"Exhausted, Hope." Levi abandoned the table he was setting up and sat across from her. "Are you okay? Last night, you were—"

"I'm so sorry about last night." Her face flushed hot as she once again remembered that something had happened last night, even if it was innocent, that she didn't recall. "I didn't mean to…well, I don't even know what happened. I was just so tired and I—"

"It's okay." He stopped her and reached for her hand. She should have pulled away, but having him touch her felt so right and natural that she couldn't bring herself to do it. "You fell asleep in the truck, and I didn't want to wake you," he said. "Well, that and I don't think I could have woken you up. You sleep hard, Hope." He laughed, but she was still too embarrassed to join in. "Seriously," he added when he realized she wasn't laughing. "You were fast asleep. I carried you upstairs and tucked you in." He squeezed her hand, and Hope had to work hard to ignore the feelings that the simple action sent racing through her. "That was it."

"That was it?"

He smiled so wide, his eyes crinkled in the corners. "Well, I might have kissed you on the forehead."

So she hadn't dreamed it.

"I couldn't help it," Levi continued. "You just looked so sweet and—"

He was cut off by the ringing of her cell phone. Tempted to hear how he finished that sentence, and then maybe the next, Hope almost let it go to voicemail. But she had a wedding in a few days, and as a rule, Hope never turned off her phone in the days leading up to a wedding. Brides were notoriously nervous, and it was her job to keep them calm. She pulled her phone out of her pocket.

It wasn't a bride.

"Excuse me for a minute." She smiled apologetically, but

Levi didn't seem bothered. He got up and resumed setting tables as Hope moved far enough away to have her conversation in private. Because from her experience, when the doctor's office called, it was rarely good news.

Levi pretended not to watch her while she took her phone call. He smoothed out the tablecloth slowly and then took his time with the steamer, moving at a fraction of the speed he'd used before Hope had joined him in the barn. It's not that her presence made him nervous—well, maybe a little—but that was only because he was afraid he would forget himself, and their history, and pull her into his arms before he could stop himself. But that wasn't why he was watching her closely.

Something was going on with her. He could feel it. There was once a time when Levi would have said that he knew her better than he knew himself. And maybe those feelings weren't totally gone because he could feel it in his bones. Something was wrong with Hope.

Across the room, she held the phone to her ear. She wasn't saying much, but he could see her nodding. She wasn't smiling. Quite the opposite.

Who was she talking to?

If they were upsetting her, he would find them and— Hope hung up the call and tucked her phone back into her pocket. Quickly, Levi tried to look busy. As if he'd done something besides stand there and stare at her while she'd been on the phone. He obviously wasn't very convincing because Hope shook her head as she walked back over to him and raised her eyebrow at the table he was working on.

He ignored the look. "Is everything okay?" He got right to the point. "The wedding isn't canceled, is it?"

"No." She shook her head and forced a smile. "It's nothing. But we have so much to do here today, we should get moving."

As if a switch had been flipped, Hope grabbed napkins and a stack of metal rings that she shoved each cloth through.

"I can do this, Hope." He hoped he sounded more confident than he was. Truthfully, he didn't know the first thing about setting a table. He'd had to watch a YouTube video earlier on how to get the wrinkles out of the tablecloth because although he hadn't known that detail, he did know enough to know that Hope would *not* be okay with wrinkles. But without more Googling, that was as far as his knowledge on setting tables went and he was pretty sure there weren't any charts in her binder with the information he needed. He'd already looked.

"No." She waved away his offer. "I got this in here. I appreciate it, but you can have the day off, Levi. I'm going to need you to come in tomorrow to accept some deliveries and be...well, just be here." She ran her hands over her face and smoothed her hair back as she obviously tried to collect her thoughts. "I have to go into the city in the morning, and it's the day before the wedding." She shook her head and looked around, presumably to take stock of what still needed to be done. "I can't leave the day before a wedding." Levi didn't respond because it was clear that she was talking to herself. "There's just too much…" She shook her head again. "But I have to. It's just going to have to—" She spun suddenly to face him, as if she'd just remembered he was there. "Can you be here tomorrow? Fridays are usually so chaotic, but there's really nothing I can do about it and I'd really appreciate—"

"Of course. Don't even worry about it. You tell me what you need, Hope. I've got it covered."

She seemed to relax a little, but still there was so much tension in her shoulders and she looked as though she might burst out in tears at any moment. Whatever it was that was bothering her, Levi wished more than anything he could take it away from her. He'd happily carry her burden so she didn't have to worry about whatever it was.

"Thank you." She smiled a little then and he felt a surge of pride go through him that at least he'd done that. And it wouldn't be the last time he made her smile. Not if he had anything to say about it. "Can you maybe get the ceremony site set up today? I don't usually do it until Friday, but...well anyway, the weather should be good and then Saturday morning we can get the speakers out and put the finishing touches on the chairs and the...did you finish the arch?"

Levi smiled. "I did. It's perfect. Do you want to see it?"

"No. I mean yes. Of course I do, but I just have..."

"You'll see it later." He hated seeing her so worked up and he knew he had no right to do it. In fact, he probably should have just kept his distance, but he could no longer stop himself. He crossed the short distance between them and pulled her into his arms.

She felt so good and at once his body responded to her familiar touch.

Caught off guard, Hope was tense at first, but it only took seconds for her to sink into the hug and let him hold her.

Levi inhaled deeply, letting the familiar scent of her fill his senses before he trusted himself enough to speak. "It's going to be okay, Hope. I'll be here for whatever you need. You take care of whatever it is you need to in the city, okay?"

She nodded against his chest but made no move to leave, which was fine with him. Because he had no plans to let her go.

"I'm here," he murmured into her ear as he swept some stray strands of hair off her cheek. It was a tender and familiar gesture, but dammit, she was so familiar and being with her, it was just...it was just right.

"Levi?" She pulled back a little so she looked up at him. "Thank you."

He couldn't find words adequate to answer her. Instead, he

cupped her cheek with one hand, bent his head, and pressed his lips to hers.

It was by a sheer act of will that his knees didn't buckle at the sweet taste of her.

Hope.

Her lips yielded under his and then, miraculously, perfectly, they were kissing him back.

Chapter Six

"I'M NOT GOING TO LIE." Faith stuffed a forkful of pasta in her mouth. "As much as I love having lunch with you, sis, it's a little strange." She shook her head and reframed what she was thinking. "Nope. It's really freaking strange."

Hope laughed a little, but her smile didn't reach her eyes.

"You *hate* coming into the city and you never come during wedding season. You don't have a booking this weekend?"

"I do."

"What?" Faith almost choked on her pasta. "Then what the hell are you doing here?"

It wasn't often that the *twin radar* went off anymore. At least not since they were kids. But when it went off, it was still just as strong. Something was definitely going on with her sister.

"I just had a few things I needed to take care of in the city, and everything is all ready for the event tomorrow. So…"

Faith tilted her head. She didn't believe her sister for a minute. "It's all ready?" She jabbed another piece of pasta with her fork and held it aloft. "You must be getting better, sis."

"I have help." Hope said it so quickly before she took a bite of her sandwich that Faith wasn't sure she'd heard it.

"Help?"

Hope nodded and Faith rolled her eyes. Clearly, her twin sister wasn't going to be as forthcoming as she would like. "What kind of help, Hope? Like you finally hired someone?"

"Something like that." She dabbed her lip with a napkin and wouldn't meet Faith's eyes. That's how she *knew* something was up.

"Spill." She stared across the table until finally Hope looked up. The moment she saw the sparkle in her sister's eye, it was confirmed. Something was definitely going on.

Hope took a deep breath and sat back in her chair. "I hired someone."

"And?"

"I hired Levi."

"Holy shit!" Faith caught her glass of water moments before it toppled over. She was vaguely aware that other diners in the restaurant were looking their way, but she didn't care. "Levi? Like, Levi, Levi?" Hope nodded. "Levi Langdon? Like, the Levi who broke your heart when he left? *That* Levi?"

Hope nodded, and this time, Faith noticed the little grin on her sister's face.

"Seriously? I mean, I knew something was up when you said his name on the phone the other day." She *knew* she should have pushed harder when Hope wouldn't tell her what Levi was doing back in town. She *knew* it. "You hired him? Why? How?"

Hope laughed and held her hand up to slow Faith down. "I know," she said. "I know. I should have told you right away. It's been crazy and so busy and..." She shrugged and dropped her hands. "I did. I hired him. Weren't you just telling me the other day that I should hire someone?"

"Not Levi!"

Hope looked around and shook her head. "Faith, people are staring."

"Let them." She fixed her wide eyes on her sister. "They *should* stare. What the actual fuck is going on? When I told you to hire someone, I certainly didn't mean for you to hire the man who crushed your heart and destroyed your dreams."

Hope rolled her eyes and picked at her sandwich. "He didn't destroy my dreams."

"But he sure crushed your heart."

Her sister shrugged. "Well, whatever you might think about it, it's actually worked out really well. He's been fantastic."

"I bet he has," Faith muttered under her breath.

"It's actually kind of crazy how fantastic it's been," she said, ignoring Faith's comment. "He built me an arch, polished floors, set up an entire room by himself, and even steamed tablecloths."

That seemed like a weird one, but Faith didn't say anything.

"And, he's actually the reason I could be here today." Was that Faith's imagination, or did her sister just blush a little bit? "He's really stepped up."

Like to be the man he should have been all those years ago?

She wanted to ask the question out loud, but she was wise enough to know that wouldn't end well.

"Besides, it's not like anything else is going to happen."

Nope. It wasn't her imagination. That was definitely a blush.

Which meant one thing…her sister was totally falling for Levi Langdon. Again.

It wasn't until after they'd finished lunch, and her sister had run off with a hug and a quick kiss, that Faith realized she hadn't actually told her why she was in the city.

She lingered outside the restaurant and contemplated calling Hope to demand an answer to her question, but ultimately, Faith didn't bother. She knew that Hope would tell her.

When she was ready, and not a moment before. After all, they did always tell each other everything.

Guilt flashed through her as she thought of Noah.

Well, maybe almost *everything.*

She amended her earlier thought. They told each other everything that was important.

And Noah wasn't an important detail. He was temporary.

Faith looked down the street toward her office and the direction she should be going before turning and walking slowly in the other direction.

No doubt the work would be piled up, waiting for when she got back, but as a paralegal, that was always the case. And no doubt she'd get in trouble. But it wasn't as if Noah could fire her. Not without it being a whole *thing*.

Everything was always a *thing* with Noah.

Faith shook her head a little. She really did have to break up with him. Of course, she'd said that before.

The thing was, she was starting to get a little worried that maybe she was actually falling for him.

And that was a problem.

With a sigh, Faith spun on her heel and headed back in the opposite direction.

The moment she walked into the office, a tingle traveled down her spine. She turned to the left, and sure enough, Noah leaned against his office door, watching her. As soon as her eyes met his, he winked and nodded his head at her.

She couldn't help but giggle and, as annoying as it was, especially to herself, Faith turned away from her office and walked toward him.

"Mr. Simmons, can I talk to you for a moment?"

"Of course, Miss Turner."

He held his arm out, welcoming her into his office, and smoothly shut the door behind him.

Faith walked straight ahead, and looked out the picture

window in front of her. The moment she heard the door click shut behind her, Faith took a deep breath.

She turned slowly, determined to tell Noah exactly what she should have told him months ago.

Faith was barely facing him when Noah's hands were on hers. And then, everything was out the window.

"You are so sexy." He kissed her hard and without hesitation, she was on him, pressing him back into the door and returning every inch of the kiss.

They crashed hard into the door and it vaguely registered that everyone in the office outside would have been able to hear that. She should have cared more than she did. Hell, she should have cared *at all*.

But when Noah kissed her—no, when he touched her, hell…when he *looked* at her—she lost all care and consideration about anything at all. Anything but him. And the way he made her feel. And that was the real reason why she hadn't broken up with him.

Her morals wouldn't let her end it over the phone or via text. And because she couldn't be alone with him long enough to tell him what she was feeling, let alone *remember* what she was feeling, they were still…doing whatever it was that they were doing.

And whatever it was that Noah was doing with his tongue on her neck… "Hmmm. That feels so good."

"*You* feel good, baby." His hands slid down her body and to the hem of her skirt, where they paused, but only for a moment. His touch on her bare skin caused a fire low in her belly. His hands slipped up her thighs, pushing her skirt up as they moved.

There were so many reasons why they shouldn't do what they were about to do, but Faith didn't care. Not enough to stop it. Her fingers found the zipper of his pants and released him into her hand. He groaned as she stroked the length of him, and then there was no going back.

Not like there was before.

Not like there *ever* was.

Noah lifted her easily, pushed her panties to one side and was inside her before she could take her next breath.

It was hot and furious, just the way she liked it.

To be fair, she liked it all the ways with Noah. She liked *all* the things about Noah.

Which was the entire problem.

No.

She pushed thoughts of what those feelings might mean from her head. There was only room for one thought and that was how good he was making her feel at that exact moment.

And that was really fucking good.

They both came quickly, but he didn't release Faith right away. Instead, Noah reached up, stroked a stray hair off her cheek, and looked directly into her eyes.

She tried to look away but his gaze held her.

Faith shook her head, silently willing him not to say anything, not to wreck what had just been a near perfect moment. But there was no help for it.

"Faith?"

She didn't answer.

He kissed her softly, sucking her bottom lip a little when he released.

"I think I'm falling in love with you."

Shit.

She squeezed her eyes shut and that's when she knew for sure.

She had to end it. For real this time.

Chapter Seven

HOPE LOVED every part of Ever After Ranch, but if she had to pick a favorite place, it would be at the far edge of her property where the river wound around the ever present pines, split and created a small island that she and Faith used to pretend was their magical place when they were kids.

The island was magical because it was *every* place. There were days when it was China and they'd traveled to the Great Wall. Logs would act as the wall and they traversed back and forth as if they were great adventurers. Some days the island was Australia, and they were backpacking through the Outback, avoiding kangaroos and venomous snakes.

Yet other days, the island was simply that—the island. A place where together they would hide from their parents and the inevitable chores they were supposed to be doing, lay on their backs in the cool grass and dream about what their futures would look like.

It had been awhile since Hope had visited the island. Life got busy; she'd grown up and instead of dreaming about her future, she was living it. She'd been so completely immersed in running the ranch and living her life that even if there'd been time to take a break and visit the island, there'd been no reason.

Until her last trip to the city.

Hope had done her best to ignore what Doctor Friesen had said to her on the phone almost two weeks ago. "Irregular results." "Run a few more tests." "Specialist." But she wasn't stupid. She knew she couldn't ignore it forever. Especially because the specialist she'd visited had used the words, "Uterine cancer."

Cancer.

She couldn't bring herself to say it out loud. She couldn't even tell Faith the real reason she'd been in town. Not that there was any point in getting her worried. In fact, she'd been feeling much better ever since she got back. She had more energy, and she hadn't had any more irregular bleeding. There was likely nothing to tell at all.

Hope pushed through the bushes along the water's edge and with nimble feet, balanced her way across the log and onto the island. She laid down on the cool grass and closed her eyes, letting the familiar sounds wash over her and clear her head. The river was still running high, after the winter runoff higher up in the mountains. Somewhere close by, a bird sang out to its mate.

She inhaled deeply and exhaled slowly, focusing as she did so on relaxing her entire body. She tried to clear her mind, and relax the underlying tension and worry she'd been holding onto. As much as Hope had tried to put the doctor's appointments out of her head so she could focus on the ranch and the weddings, random thoughts couldn't help but sneak in.

Maybe it would be easier if she'd told Faith? Or Levi?

Thinking about Levi made her smile and then all hope of trying to relax was completely out the window as thoughts of him filled her instead. The kiss they'd shared in the barn almost a week ago, and more importantly, all of the subsequent kisses since then. And there'd been a few.

She'd returned home from her city trip almost a week ago, and Levi had taken care of all the pre-wedding deliveries. In fact, the entire event had been set up exactly the way she'd asked him to, so not only was she not running around trying to make everything happen with limited time, she was actually able to enjoy herself at the festivities a little bit. Something she couldn't remember doing in a very long time.

Working with him had proved to be beneficial in more ways than one.

Hope refocused on her relaxation efforts, but it was pointless. She couldn't get Levi out of her head. With a smile on her face, Hope sat up, wrapped her arms around her knees, and stared out over the river.

She hadn't realized she'd gone to the island looking for answers of any kind, just some quiet so she could think things through. But as if the answer was delivered by the current, a decision of what to do about the impending test results came to her.

She was falling for Levi Langdon. Again. Maybe she'd never actually fallen away from him. It didn't matter, because what did matter was that maybe now that they were older, they might actually have a chance at something real.

Which was why she couldn't tell him about the doctor's appointments and tests. Not yet. Not until there was something to tell. *If* there was something to tell. She'd been feeling so much better in the last few days that she was absolutely certain that Doctor Friesen was overreacting. But either way, she wasn't going to say anything. There was no point in taking the focus off whatever it was that was happening between her and Levi. It would only cast everything in a different, more negative light, and if she was ever going to find out if there could be something real between them, nothing could get in the way.

. . .

"We're sure glad you could join us for dinner, Hope." Aunt Deb poured them each a cup of coffee before sitting down across from Levi once again. She grinned widely at her nephew and Levi shook his head with a laugh. "We've been asking and asking, but Levi keeps saying you're too busy with weddings." She fixed him with a stare and Levi shrugged. "But isn't that why you hired my long-lost nephew in the first place? If he's not pulling his weight around there, you just let me know."

Hope smiled in his direction, which had the added benefit of sending a thrill through him. "Levi's definitely helping out," she answered good-naturedly. "In fact, he's almost been *too* good."

"That's not something we're used to hearing when it comes to Levi." Logan jumped in. "Are you sure you're talking about *this* Levi?"

Levi threw his napkin at his cousin, which earned him a look of reproach from his aunt.

"I'll have you know that we're only able to be here at dinner tonight *because* I already took care of the setup for Saturday's wedding." He puffed up his chest with deserved pride. It had been a bit of a learning curve at first, but Hope had such detailed notes about what each bride wanted and how to set tables and place everything, it really wasn't much for him to show up and execute her plan. It had been a few weeks already, and Levi actually enjoyed the wedding business, something he'd never thought he'd say out loud. More importantly, he loved working with Hope.

He wasn't foolish enough to think, even for a minute, that she wasn't the entire reason he looked forward to showing up to work each and every day. That making her smile wasn't the highlight of his day. Well, maybe the kisses he tried to sneak as often as possible were the highlights of his day.

Either way, working on a fishing boat had nothing on Ever After Ranch.

"I'm sure you can't take all the credit." Katie gave Levi a look and rolled her eyes. "I think Hope probably has a pretty good handle on her business."

"She definitely does," Aunt Deb jumped in. "Word in town is that you're fully booked for the season. Is that right?"

"It is." Hope nodded and sipped her coffee. "Well, as much as I want to be. I have a few free weekends, but not many. In fact, I've been thinking of opening up to a few winter weddings next year. It'll be a lot of extra work…"

Levi didn't miss the glance she gave him. If there was work to be done, he'd be there for it.

Wouldn't he?

His mind shot to the unanswered text he'd received from his boss earlier that day. His trip to Glacier Falls was supposed to be temporary. But that was before. Before Hope.

He didn't have to make a decision yet.

Levi smiled at Hope. "I think it's a great idea. I bet you could pull off all kinds of winter wonderland things."

"Listen to you." Logan groaned and slapped his forehead, but everyone laughed. His family liked to give him a hard time, but he knew they had his back. "But hey, I just had a thought." Logan sat up, suddenly serious. "Maybe you could offer sleigh rides for the new couple?"

Hope shook her head a little. "I don't have any horses anymore. We're technically a ranch in name only."

"We have horses," Katie said. "And that really cool sleigh in the back barn. It probably could use a coat of paint."

"Or two," Logan agreed. "But Katie's right, you could use our horses."

"Absolutely," Aunt Deb jumped in. "And maybe even some of your summer brides might like a horse-drawn carriage."

Levi looked around and couldn't help but smile as his family jumped with both feet into the romantic spirit.

The rest of the evening was spent discussing the logistics of what using the horses would look like, and then, right as Levi was about to lose patience and throw Hope over his shoulder to get her out of there and get her alone, she was thanking Aunt Deb and saying goodnight to his cousins.

"That was nice," Hope said as soon as they were in his truck, driving away. "It's been awhile since I've seen your aunt. It's nice to see her doing so well."

He nodded. "I hope it wasn't too weird."

"Weird?" She turned in her seat so she faced him. "How would it be weird?"

"Well…I know…we're not…I mean, we're…" Levi shook his head with a chuckle and focused on navigating the gravel road in the dark.

She was silent for a minute, but then she asked, "We're what?"

He didn't want to have a conversation with the potential importance of this one in the truck. Not like this. He wanted to be looking at her, touching her, making damn sure that she believed everything he was telling her, without even the slightest doubt.

They were only five minutes away from Ever After Ranch.

Levi yanked the steering wheel to the right and pulled off the road. He put the truck in park, unbuckled his seat belt and was turned facing her before she could ask him again. He reached for her hand; stunned, Hope giggled a little, but let him take it into his.

"We're doing this," he said without preamble. "At least, if you want to. Because I want to. More than anything."

"This?"

"This." He used his free hand to gesture between them. "Us. This."

"This."

He nodded. "I think we can get it right this time, don't you?"

Hope laughed, but unshed tears shone in her eyes. "I think we might have a chance."

Levi scooted closer on the bench seat so he could stroke her cheek before cupping her chin gently with his fingers. "We absolutely have a chance." He looked directly into her eyes so there was no chance that she could miss what he was about to say to her. "I love you, Hope Turner. I don't think I ever quit. I made a mistake once. And I've regretted it ever since." She blinked, and a tear escaped down her cheek. He wiped it away gently. "I'm not going to make that mistake again. I love you," he said again. "Will you do this with me?"

She laughed then and finally said the words he'd been waiting to hear. "I will absolutely do this with you."

He kissed her then, and as much as he wanted that kiss to show her everything he'd just said to her, he also knew that once he started, he wasn't going to be able to stop. So he kept it as chaste as possible before pulling away, once again taking his place behind the wheel and driving like a bat out of hell the rest of the way back to Ever After Ranch. And her bed.

Hope could only laugh when he'd driven home at full speed, thrown the truck into park, and ran around to her door where he'd scooped her up. He'd kissed her there against the cool steel of the truck and he'd had to hold her up because her knees had almost completely buckled from the intensity of the kiss.

She would have happily let him have his way with her right there in the yard, but Levi clearly had other plans and they involved her bed. "Not here." His voice had been rough, only barely controlled as he tore himself away from her and took her by the hand.

Every cell in her body vibrated with anticipation. It had been years since she'd had Levi's hands on her. Sure, there'd been a few others over the years, but the reality of those other men had never been able to come close to the memory of Levi.

Somehow she managed to keep her feelings in check long enough to get the key in the lock. But the moment the door was open, he had swooped her up and inside, and he was once again kissing her up against the wall.

Her knees really didn't stand a chance against the intensity of his desire for her, and she was perfectly okay with that.

His hands were all over her and his mouth was everywhere his hands weren't. He explored every part of her over her clothes; that was a problem, because she needed his touch on her skin.

Hope wiggled back from his kiss long enough to breathe the words, "Too. Many. Clothes."

"I couldn't agree more."

Oh thank God.

But instead of stripping her clothes off, Levi scooped her up, threw her over his shoulder as if she didn't weigh anything, and charged up the stairs.

He turned to the right toward the master bedroom. For a moment, she wondered how he knew where her room was now, but then she remembered.

Levi deposited her on the bed, where she landed with a soft grunt. She rolled over and looked up at him looking down at her.

"Now, that's a sight I could never get tired of." He licked his lips and stalked toward her like a cat after his prey.

As a reflex, Hope scooted backward on the bed, her hands slipping on the comforter beneath her.

"Don't tell me you're trying to get away from me." He groaned. "I don't know if I could stand it, Hope. Honestly."

She shook her head. "Not at all."

"Good." Levi grabbed her legs and pulled her back down on the bed and then he was on top of her, straddling her with his thick, muscular thighs. "You are absolutely gorgeous." He bent to kiss her, but Hope rolled to the side and sat up.

"Remember what I said about clothes?" she asked when he looked at her in question. "Too many."

He grinned and immediately reached down to the hem of his T-shirt. A moment later, he was bare chested, and Hope had once again lost all ability to speak.

Damn! When had he gotten so damn ripped?

She didn't bother answering that, not even to herself. The last time they'd been together, they'd been barely more than kids. The man before her now was just that—a man.

A lot of man.

But he wasn't done. And there was a whole lot more man left.

Hope didn't even bother hiding her appreciation as his fingers worked at the buckle holding up his jeans and slipped those down around his ankles, where he kicked them off as well, leaving him standing completely naked in front of her.

Any chance that she might have had at formulating words vanished as she took in every hard, perfect inch of his body. Years of hard physical labor had shaped his body in all the right ways.

She couldn't help it; Hope licked her lips.

Levi groaned. "Your turn." But he shook his head, changing his mind before she could respond. "No," he said. "I want to do it."

He took a step toward her and reached for the buttons of her blouse. Her body trembled under his touch. Levi took his time, slowly pushing each button through its hole in turn.

Only once they were all unfastened did he slip his bare hands onto her shoulders and slide the fabric down, exposing her to him.

He looked her up and down appreciatively and shook his head slightly. "Hope…" He shook his head again. "No. There are no words." He bent and kissed the swell of each breast.

She tilted her head back and moaned as he slowly worked his lips over first her right breast and then her left. Slowly. Methodically.

"You're torturing me."

"That's the idea."

"Oh, no. That is most definitely *not* the idea." She grinned and put her palms on his chest. "Because I am just not that patient today." Before he could respond, she pushed gently until he fell back on the bed. Levi laughed and leaned back on his elbows with a very satisfied smile.

"But you still have far too many clothes on." His eyes roamed up and over her body, a move that made her blush from her fingertips all the way down to her toes. But she was far from shy. Especially when it came to Levi.

"I can fix that." She wanted to rip the rest of her clothes off, toss them over her shoulder and jump on him. But it was with great control that Hope moved slowly, pushing her leggings down her legs. She turned to the side and even did a little shimmy for him, a move that, judging by his reaction, had the desired effect. Still, she wasn't done. Once her pants were gone, she stood in front of him and reached around to unfasten her bra. But before she undid the clasp, Hope took her time to let her eyes travel up the length on Levi Langdon. He was both familiar and so incredibly unexpected and different that a war of emotions raged through her body.

She, too, was the same, but also so different. Hell, in only a few days, everything had changed and was likely to change even more.

Not now, Hope. She lambasted herself. It was definitely not the time to go *there.*

She blinked hard and shook her head, refocusing on the man in front of her. The *very* sexy man in front of her. Really, there was no room for thoughts of anything else. Her gaze locked onto his eyes, which were shockingly focused on hers.

"Are you almost done?"

Hope tilted her head. "Done?"

"Done overthinking this."

She laughed, but it was exactly what she needed. "I'm not overthinking anything."

"Good." He grinned and crooked his finger, beckoning her to him. "Because as much as I love looking at you, what I really want is to touch you."

Her lips twitched up. "Is that right?" Behind her back, she finally moved to unhook her bra. With the slightest shake, she let it fall to the ground.

A sound very much like a low growl came from the back of Levi's throat. "Oh, that's right."

Her panties went next, and just like that, she was done waiting and she was definitely done thinking. She crawled up, onto the bed and over him, and straddled his body. Levi's arms came up and wrapped tight around her, pulling her down to him.

Their lips met in a kiss that Hope knew right away was different. It was more intense, more passionate...more *everything.*

"I've been waiting a long time for this." Levi's words came out in a gruff breath. He'd only been back in town a few weeks, but instantly Hope knew what he was talking about.

She'd been waiting too. For years.

Their bodies moved together, their hands exploring the bodies they'd each known, and learning them all over again with touch and kisses.

When finally her impatience got the best of her, Hope wiggled against him. His hands slipped down her body until they came to rest on her hips, but Hope had other plans. She pressed up on his chest, lifting herself just a little before slowly lowering herself down onto his hard cock. She moved slowly, but still, having him inside her took her breath away. Levi froze beneath her, letting Hope grow used to him. He waited as her body quickly adjusted and she once more started moving.

"Damn, woman. You are…"

"Oh, I know." She threw her head back and laughed. But a moment later, the laughter died on her lips as her body was completely taken over by a wild tingling feeling that started deep in her core. She clenched her muscles and squirmed but Levi held her firm as a second later, the orgasm she hadn't been expecting crashed through her.

It took her a few moments to come back to herself, but when she once again opened her eyes, Levi was looking up at her, his eyes full of lust and…

"That was—"

"I'm sorry." She cut him off. "I don't know how…"

Levi's face grew serious. "Never apologize for that. It was probably the sexiest thing I've ever seen."

She probably would have blushed a little, except for his next comment. "Except, of course, looking at you right now up there, your hair all mussed, that satisfied smile on your face, knowing I put it there…damn, *that* might be the sexiest thing I've ever seen."

She shook her head, but he stopped her.

"Really, Hope. It is." He fixed her with a serious look, but then grinned as he added, "But now I really want to see which is sexier."

"Which, what?"

In answer, he wrapped one arm around her, and with strength he certainly hadn't had when they were younger, flipped them easily so he was now on top of her. He began to move inside her once more. "It's hard to choose," he said. "I like you both ways. A lot."

"Less talking." She reached up for him and pulled him down to her lips. "More kissing."

Which was exactly what they did until once more, Hope felt her orgasm build deep inside her. This time, she cried out as the sensations washed over her, and Levi joined her in his own pleasure.

Afterward, exhausted and completely satisfied, Hope drifted off to sleep tucked up tight against Levi's chest, his arm wrapped around her, keeping her safe.

Safe from everything except the phone call from the doctor the next morning that she'd somehow had managed to convince herself the evening before would never actually come.

Chapter Eight

THE CALL CAME in the next morning. But not right away. A detail that was both good and bad.

On the plus side, Hope got to wake up in Levi's arms, pulled tight up against his body. A body that had spent the entire night loving her, and judging by what was pressed up against her back, was ready to love again. Morning sex was leisurely and lazy and oh so good, before Levi finally slipped away from her and left her to get ready for her day.

That was definitely the plus side.

The downside of not getting the call until she was sipping her coffee and flipping through notes about a bride who couldn't decide on the music for her ceremony and wanted Hope to help her decide was that, by that time, Hope had completely forgotten about the impending phone call at all.

That changed the second the ring of her cell phone jarred through her internal debate on a popular country song for the walk down the aisle, or a less known instrumental accompaniment. In that instant, in vivid detail, she remembered.

For a moment, Hope stared at her phone and the flash of the incoming call and froze.

It could be good news.

She let it ring.

Maybe it could just go to voicemail.

The table vibrated under the phone.

Dammit.

Hope snatched up her cell and pushed the button to answer the call. "Hope Turner, Ever After Ranch."

"Hope? This is Doctor Friesen."

She knew *that.*

"Hi, Doctor Friesen." She forced a cheerfulness into her voice despite the pit of dread that had settled into the pit of her stomach. "What can I help you with this morning?" *Maybe if she denied it to herself a little bit longer, it would all go away.*

But of course it wouldn't.

"I wanted to call you myself, Hope." The doctor got right to the point. "The test results have come back." He paused and that's when she knew with certainty. She wasn't going to like what he was about to tell her. "It's cancer. I'm sorry, Hope."

Cancer.

She didn't hear anything else the doctor had to say because the only thing she could hear was that word. Cancer. *Cancer.* CANCER.

It roared in her head, bouncing around her brain until finally—silence.

It took her a second to remember she was on the phone with Doctor Friesen and he had clearly just said something. "I'm sorry," she muttered before she realized how ridiculous it was for her to be apologizing given the circumstances.

"I understand," he said kindly. "There's no good way to get that news, Hope. I really am sorry. But I don't believe in calling you in to meet with me to get the results when you need to know as soon as possible."

She nodded despite the fact that he couldn't see her. "That makes sense."

"Okay. Now if you're sitting down, we can go over a few things, okay?"

Once more, she nodded.

For the next few minutes, Hope scribbled down bits and pieces of information as she tried to process what the doctor was telling her.

Uterine cancer.

Early stages.

Excellent prognosis.

Treatment.

So it wasn't *all* bad. Maybe if there was a kind of cancer that you *had* to have, this one wasn't so bad. The idea was laughable, and not because she thought it was even remotely funny.

How could there possibly be a good *kind of cancer?*

"I've set up an appointment with the specialist in the city for tomorrow."

"Tomorrow?"

"I think it's best that you get in to see Doctor Barrett. She'll be able to talk you through the next steps."

"The next steps?"

He paused on the other end of the line before speaking again. "I hesitate to speak on this, Hope, because Doctor Barrett really is the best, but..."

"But, what?"

"You're young and otherwise very healthy and I'm sure she will advise you the same way I would."

She swallowed hard. Doctor Friesen had been her doctor for her entire life; she trusted him. "What's that?"

"Typically with cancers of this nature, the protocol is to perform a hysterectomy to give the patient the best possible prognosis."

Hysterectomy.

"Like I said," the doctor continued. "I'm sure Doctor

Barrett will be able to go over the options with you more specifically, but I just wanted you to hear it from me."

Hope nodded. "I appreciate that," she answered honestly.

"And Hope?"

She didn't answer before the doctor continued.

"I'm really sorry it couldn't be better news."

You and me both.

It was a beautiful day in the mountains. The sun shone through the crispness of a mountain morning, with the promise of being a warm afternoon. It was Levi's favorite time of the year in Glacier Falls because the snow was gone, but it wasn't yet so hot that the days got lazy.

It was a perfect morning in late May.

Of course, it didn't hurt that he'd spent the night in Hope's bed. No, that didn't hurt at all.

If he'd had his way, he'd still be in her bed, wrapped around her or on top of her, or under her, or really anything as long as he was with her. Damn, he'd missed that woman more than he'd realized. Being with her was both familiar and brand freaking new and he couldn't get enough.

Unfortunately for him, Levi hadn't gotten his way, and they both had work to do, so he'd reluctantly slipped out of her bed and gone back to the Langdon ranch to shower and change as quickly as he could. He planned to stop by the bakery in town to pick up a few of their delicious chocolate chip muffins that Hope used to love. And he had other plans, too.

The night before, neither of them had gotten much sleep. Besides the mind-blowing sex—seriously, what *had* he been missing?—they'd also talked. *Really* talked.

Cuddled up in bed, Hope's smooth, soft back pressed up against his chest, he'd told her about the places he'd traveled to over the last few years. Mostly his trips involved the coast, and fishing, but the money he'd earned on the boats had allowed him the opportunity to explore parts of the world that had always been little more than a dream. He'd been to Costa Rica, Ireland and Scotland, Australia, and to more states and provinces than he could count.

Hope, on the other hand, hadn't been anywhere.

At first, Levi had reacted with shock, but it made sense. After her parents died, she'd dedicated her entire life to getting Ever After Ranch off the ground. And she'd done it, too. Hard work, long hours, and a complete devotion to her business had definitely resulted in success. But that success had come at the expense of seeing the world.

The idea occurred to Levi sometime right before dawn. He'd woken early, and unwilling to fall back asleep, he'd spent the time before the sun rose in the sky letting her silky hair run through his fingers, and thinking about how he could pull off the ultimate surprise.

He was going to take Hope on a trip. Nothing elaborate. At least not yet. But it would have a beach, because the idea of spending a week alone with Hope in a bikini sounded pretty damn appealing.

As soon as he was finished in the shower, Levi grabbed Logan's laptop from the little desk in the kitchen where he always kept it and settled in at the table with a cup of coffee to begin his search. Right away, he narrowed down his choices to an all-inclusive resort. There would be plenty of times to do some more adventurous exploring, but for their first trip together, he wanted it to be easy. So all they had to focus on was each other.

First trip together.

Levi laughed out loud at how easily he'd assumed that there would be more trips. He'd gone from zero to sixty with Hope, and he wasn't about to start making apologies for it because it felt right. More right than anything he'd ever done.

"What's so funny?" Logan walked into the kitchen and poured himself a cup of coffee. "Is that my laptop?"

"I left mine at the barn." Levi hardly looked up. "I needed to take care of something before I headed back to the ranch. Figured you wouldn't mind."

Logan shrugged and sat across from him at the table. "So what's so funny?"

"I'm just laughing at myself," he answered honestly. "I'm just trying to sort out some plans for…well, for—"

"You and Hope?" Levi looked up from the screen and stared at his cousin, who grinned. "What?" Logan asked casually. "You don't think we all noticed that you didn't come home last night?" He tipped his head in question but only laughed when Levi didn't answer. "Hey," Logan said. "You don't have to answer to me. Besides, it's not like any of us are surprised."

"Except me." Katie walked into the room and both men turned to look at her in surprise. "Okay, I'm not really," she confessed. "I'm actually more surprised that she took you back, if I'm being honest. I mean, you kind of left."

Guilt flashed through Levi. It wasn't the first time he'd felt terrible about the way his younger self had handled things and it was sure to not be the last time either.

Before he could reply, Logan answered for him. "Well, even the smartest women make poor choices sometimes." He winked at Levi across the table.

Hope hadn't been the only thing he'd missed. Levi had missed his cousins, his family, a lot.

"Either way," Katie said. "I'm happy for both of you." She wrapped an arm around him and squeezed. "What are you looking at? Mexico? Nice! Is that where you're going next?"

"Next?"

"Didn't you say you were going back to work on the boat?" She shrugged and pulled out a seat at the table. "I don't know, do you fish in Mexico?"

"You can," he said. "But I don't."

"But you *do* fish?" Logan asked. "Look, I'm not trying to chase you away, Levi. Quite the opposite. I actually like having you around, but you did say that you were just visiting. Has that changed?"

Both his cousins looked at him, waiting for an answer.

And he wanted to give them one. Especially because up until that exact moment, he'd managed to forget that his trip to Glacier Falls was in fact meant to be temporary. Just a side trip while the boat he'd been working on underwent some repairs. A few weeks, the summer at most, before he went back. Somehow, he'd managed to forget all that and slip right back into life in town as if he'd never left.

"Levi?" Katie watched him carefully. "Are you staying?"

"I want to," he answered honestly. "But you're right. It was only supposed to be temporary, so I guess I'll have to work out a few details."

Not the least of which would be finding different work. He enjoyed working for Hope at the ranch—for so many reasons —but it didn't pay very much. And besides that, it was only temporary for the busy wedding season. He was used to making a good living on the fishing boats, and although he had a bit of savings, it wouldn't last long if he didn't secure regular work. And then, of course, there was Hope. Hope was the big one. Would she want him to stay? He was pretty sure of the answer on that, but it wouldn't hurt to talk to her about it first, just to make sure they were on the same page the way he hoped like hell they were.

And then there was the small, but very important detail of his boss. The owner of the fishing company he'd worked for called again the night before, and of course Levi had let it go to voicemail. He'd left Levi a message that only a few short weeks ago would have been the best thing he could have heard. He'd offered Levi his very own boat.

Him. A captain.

It had been a dream of his for years, since he was a deck hand on his first vessel. It wasn't that Levi loved to fish. It was more that he'd always aspired for more. And now he had the chance to grab it.

Levi glanced again at the screen full of beach holidays in front of him before closing the laptop lid and looking at his cousins. "Yes," he said. "I have a few things to work out."

"Becky, it will be okay," Hope said for at least the dozenth time. "I promise, adding a flower girl at the last minute won't be a problem. Not at all." Hope made a mental note to check with her friend who worked at Glacier Falls High for some babysitter recommendations for this surprise flower girl after the ceremony.

"I'm so sorry, Hope." Becky, who was getting married in only a few short days, looked the very opposite of a glowing bride at that moment. She'd showed up unexpectedly about forty minutes earlier and had been crying and panicking about almost every detail for her special day ever since. They'd already gone over the centerpieces, the music, the place settings, the seating arrangement, and now were on to the unexpected addition of having her five-year-old niece as the flower girl.

"It will be perfect," Hope reassured the woman again. "I'm sure she'll be absolutely adorable. I'll give her a little basket full of flower petals that she can scatter. Super easy, and she shouldn't need any help. Does that sound okay?"

Becky nodded, but instead of smiling, she broke out in tears. Hope moved swiftly to get the woman a box of tissue. She'd dealt with her fair share of overwhelmed brides, but it had been awhile since she'd had one as emotional as Becky. "That doesn't sound okay?" Hope asked tentatively.

"No," the other woman said between sniffles. "It sounds good. It does and she's super cute and I love her. It's just…"

"What's going on?" Hope led Becky to a nearby bench and sat down next to her. "What can I do to make things better for you?"

It was an innocent question, one that should have helped relive some of the stress, but instead it only made her cry harder. Hope waited her out and finally Becky blew her nose and said, "There's nothing you can do. It's all such a mess."

Alarm bells went off. In her career, Hope had only had three brides call off their wedding at the last minute, and it usually started with something like what Becky had just said. She took a deep breath. "I'm sure it's not so bad."

"It is! I'm pregnant!"

Hope felt as if she'd been punched in the gut. She'd managed to put off all thoughts of the call she'd had with Doctor Friesen a few hours earlier, but the mention of a baby brought it all rushing back with a clarity that made her want to throw up.

Baby.

Her eyes instinctively went to the other woman's stomach.

Baby.

Becky was talking, but all Hope could focus on was her belly and the life growing in there. *Would she ever have the same? Would she one day have a child? A baby of her own?*

Ever since she was a little girl, Hope had wanted a child of her own one day. Maybe twins if she was lucky. She'd never considered the possibility that she might not ever be able to see that dream become a reality.

Until now.

Her hands went to her own stomach. Something was growing inside her, all right, but it wasn't a child she would hold and love and raise. It was a terrible disease that was slowly threatening her very existence, never mind any of the dreams that she might have so foolishly believed were untouchable.

Tears pricked at her eyes.

"Hope?"

Becky's voice brought her right back into the moment in a flash. She blinked hard and wiped at her face.

"Hope? Are you all right?" Becky's face had morphed from one of stress and overwhelm into one of distinct concern. "You don't look well."

Hope took a deep breath and forced a smile to her face. "I'm fine." She had to stay in control. Her personal crisis wasn't going to change anything for this bride, and her special day was only a few short days away. Hope would remain professional and do her very best to make sure it went off without a hitch. "Sorry, I don't know what just happened there. But yes, I'm fine." She reached for Becky's hand and squeezed. "Now, tell me why being pregnant is going to ruin everything because I think it's absolutely wonderful." She swallowed hard to keep her own feelings from taking over.

Becky gave her one last concerned look, but ultimately, her own concerns took precedence. "My mom is going to freak out if she finds out that I got pregnant before the wedding. She's so old-fashioned. She almost had a heart attack when I told her that Phillip and I were going to live together before we got married. I don't want her to say anything or ruin the wedding or anything because of it."

Hope couldn't help but smile. "This is an easy one," she said. "Just don't tell her. After all, will it make a difference if you let her know before Saturday, or can it wait a little bit longer?"

"It can wait."

"Of course it can. And I'll make sure the staff knows that you won't be drinking any champagne. I'll have some sparkling apple juice brought in just for you, and you and Phillip can keep it a secret." Becky started to visibly relax. "In fact, it will be kind of special, don't you think? In a way, your little one will be with you on your special day."

Becky's hands went to her stomach and she smiled so broadly, Hope knew she was on board. "That's perfect," she said. "Thank you, Hope. I'm so sorry I got so freaked out. I'm just so overwhelmed with everything and—"

"Don't give it anymore thought. That's why I'm here. I'll take care of everything, okay?"

Becky nodded. They discussed a few more details and then she left so Hope could finish the preparations.

It was only after she was alone that Hope allowed herself to think once more about what Doctor Friesen's words had really meant.

Cancer.

Hysterectomy.

Both of which meant one thing—no chance at children.

And what did *that* mean for her? Her future? Her—

"Hope?"

She spun at her name and her body responded with a reflexive warm flush at the sight of Levi. But the warmth didn't last long as the reality of what she was now facing would no doubt affect him and what she had allowed herself to think for even a minute could be something special.

Chapter Nine

"I WISH you would have told me about this earlier. You shouldn't have had to worry about this on your own. Not for even one second." Her sister gave her a hug the moment she saw her, and instantly Hope felt better. Faith was right; she *should* have told her earlier. And maybe she should feel guilty about not telling her twin sister about the health scare that had brought her into the city previously, or even about the tests she'd been waiting for results on. And maybe there was part of her that did feel a little guilty about that. But truthfully, she really hadn't actually believed there was anything to get worked up about, so she hadn't said anything.

Until the night before when she'd called her sister and asked her to take the afternoon off work to be with her for a very important doctor's appointment. More specifically, the oncologist appointment that was without a doubt going to change her life.

"I'm sorry," she mumbled into her sister's shoulder.

"Don't be. I'm here now and you are *not* going to face any of this alone. I've got you." She pulled back and stared Hope in the eyes. "For everything. I'm here and I'm not going anywhere."

The tears that had been threatening to spill for the last twenty-four hours couldn't be held back any longer. Hot, wet tears streamed down Hope's cheeks. Faith gathered her up in another hug and squeezed again, holding on until Hope's tears dried up. At least temporarily.

"Are you ready to do this?"

Hope nodded. "The sooner I know what's up, the better it will be."

"I agree."

Together they walked through the glass doors into the clean, and almost cold, office of Doctor Barrett, where an overly cheerful receptionist greeted them in a singsong voice and small talk about how beautiful the weather was before telling them to have a seat and help themselves to coffee or water while they waited. Hope bit back a sarcastic comment about how it was far from a beautiful day considering she was there in the office where she was about to hear all about her *cancer* and certainly there could be nothing *beautiful* about that at all, but Faith led her across the room and sat her down before she could say anything.

"Someone should probably remind that woman where she works," Faith said before rolling her eyes.

It made Hope laugh out loud and she was actually smiling a moment later when a nurse called her name.

She wasn't smiling ten minutes later, however, when Doctor Barrett, who turned out to be a lovely woman in her forties with a kind but no-nonsense approach, told her the specifics of the type of cancer that Hope had. Most of what she said was a blur. Thankfully, Faith was taking notes on her phone next to her because Hope didn't have a prayer to remember everything.

Finally, they got to the nitty-gritty. "Because the cancer was caught early, there are a few choices on how you would like to proceed now."

"Choices?" Hope sat up straight. "I assumed that you'd have to..." She couldn't bring herself to say it out loud. Not yet.

"A hysterectomy?"

Hope nodded.

"It *is* an option," the doctor said. "And honestly, in my opinion, it's a very good one. With a hysterectomy, we can remove the cancerous cells in their entirety and because you're still in an early stage, hopefully that will be enough for a long term, possibly permanent remission."

"That sounds good." Faith looked between Hope and the doctor. "Why not just sign up for that? I mean, if it can get rid of the cancer...there's no other choice."

"There is," Doctor Barrett said kindly. She looked to Hope, who was trying as hard as she could not to break down in front of her. "You're quite young still and often younger patients like to consider another option. One that will allow them the possibility of having children."

Hope's stomach clenched and she nodded slowly.

"If that's something you would like to consider, we can treat you in the short term with hormone therapy, allowing time for a healthy pregnancy before taking more permanent measures."

Hope released the breath she'd been holding and almost smiled. "You mean, I could still have a baby?"

"There is a—"

"But won't that give the cancer a chance to get worse?" Faith interrupted. "Is it worth the risk?" Her face was lined with worry.

"It's a lot to think about," the doctor said before Hope could answer. "Which is why I want you to give it some thought. Do you have a partner or significant other in your life?"

Levi.

"I...um...well..."

The doctor smiled softly. "If it's appropriate, may I suggest that you discuss it with him?" Hope nodded numbly. "Okay, let's set up an appointment next week to discuss your decision and next steps. Either way, we will need to move forward on treatment as soon as possible. If you need to take time off work, or—"

"I run my own business."

"This might be a good time to make sure you have help. No matter which route you choose, you will need a lot of support."

"She's got me." Faith grabbed her hand, giving her strength.

"I meant what I said earlier," Faith told her sister later when they'd finally finished up at the doctor's office and sat on a park bench, looking out over the river. It was the same river that wound through Ever After Ranch before it found its way down the mountains and into the city. The rushing water had calmed Faith when she was feeling a little homesick for the mountain home she'd always been in such a hurry to leave. There were some things she missed terribly about her hometown. "You've got me," she said to Hope, who stared out over the river. "For whatever you need. You're not doing this alone."

Hope nodded.

"I mean, I know that you're not alone," Faith added. "You have Levi, I guess. I mean, I don't really know what's going on there, but—"

"No," Hope interrupted her. She turned to face her sister. "I need you, Faith." Her sister looked at her so intensely that it took a great deal of strength for Faith not to break down. From the moment Hope had called to let her know what was going on and that there was a specialist appointment that she needed her to accompany to, Faith had wanted to break down. And not necessarily in tears. But with yelling, screaming, and...okay, probably tears.

She would *not* lose her sister. No way.

"I'm here," Faith said. "For whatever you need. I got you, sis." She reached over and took her sister's hand but couldn't look at her. If she did, she would for sure cry, and Hope didn't need that right now. She needed her to be strong. Faith had always been the stronger of the two, while Hope was more caring or more *sensitive.*

"I need you to come home with me."

Except that.

She closed her eyes and inhaled deeply, letting the sounds of the river wash over her.

Fuck.

"Faith?"

She nodded.

"You'll come home with me?"

One more deep breath. There really was no other choice. "Of course."

Next to her, Hope sighed audibly. "Thank goodness. Because I have such a busy season and I don't know how I would do it on my own. I mean, I'm not on my own, but I can't really ask Levi, well...I don't know yet what I can and can't do. But I'm going to—"

"Hope?" Faith turned to face her sister finally as she bit her bottom lip to keep from tearing up. "I told you, I've got you. And I'll take care of the business if that's what you need me to do. I'll hold your hand, I'll bring you tea and sandwiches, I'll watch movies all day with you and sit with you for...for whatever. Okay? You're not alone. You'll never be alone as long as I'm around."

As she spoke, Faith forced herself not to think about what would happen if Hope didn't beat this. About the fact that it would be *her* who would be alone. But there was no time to think of anything but Hope and what she would need.

"Have you thought about your options?" She hated to ask because as far as Faith was concerned, there were no options. There was *the* option. But she also knew that wasn't how her sister worked.

Hope nodded and the tiniest of smiles twitched at her lips and that's when she knew.

Hope had already made her choice.

And it was the wrong one.

She didn't mean to, but a noise that sounded disturbingly like the sound that their mother used to make when she was disappointed with something they'd done slipped out of her lips.

Instantly, Hope straightened her spine and shook her head. "I don't expect you to understand, Faith. But…well, look, I don't want to discuss it right now. I really should get back to the ranch. We have a wedding this weekend and—"

Faith put a hand on her sister's arm as she stood to leave. "I'm sorry," she said when her sister finally looked down to her. "I really am. I promise I won't say a thing. Whatever you want. I'm only here to support you."

Hope looked as if she might say something else, but after a moment she nodded and pulled her up into a hug. "Thank you," Hope muttered against her shoulder. "I really don't know what I'd do without you."

"Well, you don't have to worry about it." Faith put a smile on her face that she knew didn't reach her eyes. "Now, get out of here and get back to the ranch." She forced a small laugh. "If I'm going to go and help you out for a while, I'll have to take care of a few things." She shook her head a little as the mental list of what she was going to have to do grew in her mind. "Noah is going to be pissed."

"Noah?" Hope gave her a side eye. "You've never mentioned a Noah before."

She shrugged as casually as she could before turning to go. "I guess I'm not the only one who can keep secrets."

"What do you mean you're leaving?"

Faith had known Noah wouldn't respond well to the news that she was going to take a leave of absence. Of course, if she was honest with herself, she hadn't expected him to be quite as worked up as he was.

She'd waited until after the workday was over, and she'd had a chance to discuss it with the HR department. Fortunately, her company had a very generous policy regarding family issues and combined with all of her unused holiday time, she should be able to take as much time off as she needed to be with Hope.

Which was the most important thing. The fact that ever since she'd told Noah when he'd arrived at her condo less than twenty minutes ago, he'd been following her around and peppering her with questions, wasn't going to distract her from what was important.

"I told you, Noah." Faith opened her closet and dug through her business suits to find something that would be appropriate for wedding planning. "I need to be there for Hope right now." *What did one wear to plan a wedding?* She laughed at herself, as if what to wear was the biggest problem she was going to have when it came to planning a wedding.

"What's so funny?" Noah leaned up against the closet door and crossed his arms over his chest. "Is this funny to you some-how? That you're leaving me with no warning at all? What about the accounts you're working on? The clients? Is everyone supposed to pick up the slack just because you decide to run off to the mountains?"

Faith spun around, a selection of blouses and dress pants in her hands. "That's what this is about? Work? You're more worried about the stupid firm than my sister's life?" She pushed past him to the bed, where she tossed down the clothes.

"No!" He was right behind her. "That's not it, Faith. That's not what I'm saying."

She shot him a look over her shoulder. "Really? Because that sounds exactly like what you're saying."

"Faith, I'm trying to understand how you can just put everything on hold and run back to the mountains, all in the span of a few hours."

"I told you, my sister is sick. She needs me."

"I don't know if she needs you to put your entire life on hold."

"She does." There was no way he was going to understand it. Nor did Faith care about trying to get him to understand. She had too much to do. "Besides, it isn't your choice."

"I get that."

Faith hesitated for a second. She knew she was being cold-hearted and distant. But she couldn't help it. Not really. Hell, she certainly hadn't expected when she woke up that morning that only a few hours later she'd be packing her bags and leaving her job and...well, *him*...to head back to Glacier Falls. But sometimes life didn't work out the way you thought it would. Besides, she'd been meaning to break up with Noah for ages. If she'd been looking for a sign of some kind, she couldn't really think of a better one. She swallowed hard and kept packing. If she turned around, if she let herself look at him or *feel* anything...well, there was no reason to make things any harder than they needed to be.

"But it just doesn't make sense," Noah continued. "You

always say that you'd never go back to your hometown, that you were made for city life. And working for your sister? In *weddings?*" Faith couldn't help but cringe when he said it out loud because she knew exactly why it didn't make any sense to him. The same way it wouldn't have made any sense to her. "You always tell me how ridiculous your sister's business is. Hell, Faith. You make fun of it! You've told me yourself, you don't believe in happily ever after. How the hell are you supposed to *sell* it?"

Everything Noah said was true. And if she wasn't already so conflicted about it, she might agree with him. But she'd promised Hope, and she wasn't about to go back on her word. Especially when her sister needed her.

She moved past Noah into her bathroom and gathered her toiletries together. "I'll just have to figure out a way to get past all that." Her words didn't sound very convincing, even to her own ears. "I get that you don't understand it, Noah, but I don't need to explain it to you." She turned to face him with a hairbrush in one hand and a bottle of lotion in the other. "I'm going back to Glacier Falls and I'm going to help my sister create happily ever afters for a handful of couples who have bought into the whole love thing and it's going to be fine. More than fine."

Maybe if she said it enough, she'd start to believe it herself. Because frankly, the whole idea of having to live on the ranch in a small town in the middle of nowhere and help happy couples experience their most perfect romantic day, all while caring for her sick sister who absolutely could not die on her, sounded like hell.

"It'll be okay," she said again. "And the firm will just have to deal without me."

"I'm sure we'll sort it out," Noah said. "Your clients will... never mind. It'll be fine."

Faith knew it would. She wasn't that integral to the day-today operations. No doubt, in less than a week, the rest of the associates would absorb her case load and it would be as if she'd never even been there. She knew the drill. She'd seen it happen before when women went on maternity leave. Taking an extended leave from the firm was essentially career suicide. Unless, of course, you didn't mind starting over at the bottom when—or if—you ever came back. She knew that very well.

Faith looked carefully at the man in front of her. He was always dressed so sharply in an expensive, well-cut suit, his hair perfectly in place. She knew what was under that crisp linen shirt and it was a rock-hard chest, honed from hours in the gym. Noah took care of himself. He was sexy as hell and just looking at him sent chills through her. She shook her head slowly and forced herself to look away.

"Faith?"

She stopped and took a deep breath before turning around again.

"This isn't about the firm," he said slowly. "You know that, right?"

She didn't answer. She was too busy trying to control her breathing. *Why did he have to make this so fucking hard?*

"And it's not about you going to work in a business you don't believe in," he continued. "Although, I'm not going to pretend to understand it." He laughed a little, but Faith was too busy trying to keep her body from shaking to join in.

His laughter trailed off. Noah shook his head and looked down at his feet for a moment before trying again. "You make this really difficult, you know?"

"Pardon?" Faith stood her ground. "What exactly am I making difficult? Because I'm just trying to—"

He cut her off with a kiss. Both hands pressed to her cheeks, holding her in place, she was completely taken off guard. For a split second, Faith almost let herself melt into it, but then her senses came back to her in a crash. Her brush and lotion still in her hands, she brought them to Noah's chest and shoved him backward. "What are you doing?" She took a step back, needing distance between them. "Noah, I don't—"

"Seriously?" Noah's fingers went to his lips before he took a step toward her. "I'm trying to show you how I—"

"Well, don't." She charged past him to the duffel bag on the bed and shoved a few more things inside before zipping it up with a violent tug. "Don't tell me or show me or…just don't."

He put his hand on her arm. "Faith, you—"

"No." She shrugged it off. But she couldn't look at him because if she did, she knew she'd be lost. The truth was, she'd been trying and failing to break it off with him for so long because she really didn't want to. She *liked* Noah. *Really* liked him. He was successful, handsome, caring, and an amazing lover. He was everything. And more than that, he seemed to really like her, too.

And *that* was the problem. She might have to go home and play make-believe wedding planner in a fairy-tale world for a little while, but that didn't change anything.

She still didn't believe in love. Or marriage. Or forever. And letting herself pretend, even for a moment, that it might be possible would only end in heartbreak.

Faith straightened her shoulders and turned around. "Noah, I can't see you anymore."

Chapter Ten

IT WAS another successful wedding for Ever After Ranch, as if Levi had any doubts. He'd only been there a few weeks, and it hadn't even taken that long to see that Hope ran a well-oiled machine. Every event was unique and different, but every single one had gone off without a hitch. Except, of course, for the usual minor mishaps and issues, but none of those little details turned out to be a big deal, due largely to Hope and her brilliant organization. It really was an impressive thing to watch her in action.

And it was because of her planning and the way she'd set things up that allowed Levi to help out the way he did. He wasn't foolish enough to actually take any of the credit himself. It was all Hope. Every bit of it. She was amazing.

He leaned against the wooden beam and watched her in action. She floated around the room, just on the fringes, not interfering with the festivities in any way. Orchestrating every-thing seamlessly. She was gorgeous in her tailored navy dress, her blonde hair secured in a clip at the back of her head. She'd perfected the art of blending in while absolutely standing out. At least to him, because he only had eyes for her.

Levi had tried more than once to get her alone since their memorable night together, but she'd been so busy, and then there was another last-minute trip to the city, which meant that not only had a lot of the last-minute prep work fallen to him again, but that when Hope did return to the ranch, she was far too busy to be able to spend any time with him.

If it were any other circumstance, Levi might be a little bit jealous, but he knew how hard she worked and how much pride she took in what she did. It was one of the reasons he loved her.

Maybe it should have felt strange to even think that way so easily after all this time, but it didn't. It felt so very right.

And why shouldn't it?

After all, it wasn't the first time that he'd felt this way about Hope Turner.

Correction—it absolutely was the first time he'd felt this way. He'd loved her before, that was certain. But this was different. *Very* different. More intense, more *real*.

Levi let his gaze drift back to Hope, watching her in action. Only there was something different, something he couldn't quite put his finger on. It was in the way she moved, the way she held her back, a little stiffer than normal. He hadn't seen her more than a few minutes in the last few days, and he hadn't noticed anything off about her then, but something was definitely off.

As soon as Hope turned around, he saw the reason for his confusion. Hope wasn't Hope. She was Faith.

He laughed a little under his breath. When was the last time he'd mixed the two of them up? It had to have been years. High school, maybe. The Turner twins had always been so different, despite their almost identical appearance, he'd almost always been able to tell them apart. Probably because he'd only ever been in love with one of them.

There was that word again.

Love.

Levi shook his head and let a smile spread over his face as he watched Faith. She really was so different from her sister. The long blonde hair, brilliant blue eyes, and curvy figure—those were all the same, but that's where the similarities ended. Everything else about them was totally opposite. Hope loved the idea of love and everything that went with it. She'd always been the *softer* of the two, while Faith had become hard and jaded. Hope never could tell him why it was, only that something had changed when they were teenagers and her sister had declared one day that she didn't believe in any of it. And never again wanted to dress up like one of the *wedding sisters*, the way they had since they were little, because she couldn't be part of something that was so clearly a sham.

As soon as she could, Faith had left home for the city and as far as Levi knew—which, to be fair, wasn't *all* the information—had rarely been home since.

Which was why it was extraordinarily unexpected that she stood in the middle of the wedding festivities, holding a clipboard and looking like she was…working?

Something was really off and he was about to find out what exactly it was when Hope appeared by her sister's side. She was dressed almost identically, and when she arrived next to Faith, her sister looked visibly relieved. They shared a few words and Hope took the clipboard from her hand and made a few notes, while Faith disappeared into the kitchen.

He watched her go before pushing up from where he leaned to make his way over to Hope. This time, sure it was her, he slipped his hands around her waist and pulled her close into his chest for a quick peck on the cheek before letting her go. Professionalism was important to her, and as much as he wanted to wrap her up in his arms and kiss her hard to show her exactly what he'd been thinking of since he'd slipped from her bed the other day, he resisted.

Barely.

"Hey." Levi pulled away. "I've missed you."

"I've missed you, too." She gave him a smile, but it didn't quite reach her eyes. "The last few days have just been so busy, I hardly even know what day it is."

"It's Saturday." Levi gave her a cocky wink. "Wedding day, remember?"

"Of course." Her blush slipped up and over her ears. "I just meant—"

"I know what you meant." He reached for and found her hand. "I'm just giving you a hard time." Levi waited for her smile to return before he asked the next question. "What's Faith doing here?" Hope pulled her hand away from his and tucked it up around her clipboard. "I'm not going to lie," he continued, ignoring the change in her demeanor. "I was surprised to see her. It's been—"

"Years," she finished for him. "I know. I asked her to come help me out for a little bit."

"Help you out?" He didn't even try to hide the shock from his voice. "With what?"

"The ranch." She wouldn't meet his eyes.

"You don't need help, Hope."

He felt a flash of guilt at telling her what she did or did not need with her business, but he couldn't help it. She *didn't* need help. She had him.

"I do." She turned to look at him then. "I mean, I know you're here, Levi, and I appreciate your help with everything *so* much. Everything has run so much smoother since you've been here. It really has. But—"

"But, what?" He knew what she was going to say, and for more reasons than he could articulate at that moment, he didn't want to hear it. Any of it.

"But I know you're going to leave," she finished. "You have

a whole life away from here and I can't expect you to put it all on hold for me and—"

Levi knew it was unprofessional; he knew that Hope would probably be angry with him later, but it didn't matter. Without missing a beat, he took her hand back and swirled her onto the dance floor where he could get her alone, with her full attention on him. And that's exactly what he wanted, too. At least until he finished saying exactly what it was that he needed to say.

"Levi! What are you doing?"

Hope relented as he took the clipboard from her hand and put it on a nearby table as he wrapped his arm around her, clasped her other hand, and guided her into an easy waltz on the side of the dance floor.

"We can't do—"

"We can, too. Everything is going smoothly, everyone else is dancing, and we're in the corner. No one can see us."

It was true and even though she would never normally take a personal moment during an event, she gave in and let Levi lead her.

He must have seen the surrender on her face because he grinned and spun her before pulling her in close again.

"I have a surprise for you."

It wasn't what she'd expected him to say, not at all.

"A surprise?"

"Yes." He smiled so wide, Hope couldn't help it; in that moment, she forgot everything. The doctor's appointment, the terrible diagnosis, the even worse diagnosis, and despite herself, she giggled. "Do you want to know what it is?"

"Of course." She felt like a teenager again as the anticipation grew.

"I got us two tickets to Mexico."

Hope froze in mid-step, coming to a stop so suddenly that Levi tripped over her and almost stumbled before catching himself. "Mexico?"

The room spun, or maybe it was the dancers enjoying themselves all around her. Either way, she had to get off that dance floor. Hope glanced around, looking for an escape, but Levi held her fast. "Mexico," he repeated.

"But why?"

Levi had wrapped his arms around her again and had tried to start moving to the music—a slightly faster song—again, but Hope was no longer feeling it, and she stumbled over his feet until finally he stopped and held her instead. "Because we were just talking about seeing the world, Hope." He looked at her so earnestly it brought tears to her eyes. "I told you I'd show you the world, Hope. And I meant it."

He *had* said that. At the time she'd believed him, too. Had it really just been the other day laying in his arms that he'd told her that? Just the other day that the world still seemed so fair? That she had her whole life ahead of her?

Shit.

"I can't go." She didn't even realize she'd said the words out loud until she saw the look on his face. "I mean, I want to…I just…"

"Of course you can."

"No." She shook her head. "I can't."

All traces of his earlier smile were gone now. "Why?" he asked with a shake of his head. "Why can't you go? I looked at the calendar. I booked the tickets for fall—you don't have anything scheduled. We can just block it off. We can—"

"No. It's not that. I just…" She couldn't tell him the real reason. She knew that in a flash just by looking at his face. She couldn't tell him she was sick and she definitely couldn't tell him that she'd decided without a doubt that she was going to try for a baby. There was no way she could travel. For so many reasons. But if she told him any of them, he'd…well, she didn't know what he would do. But whatever it was, it wouldn't be fair to him. It wouldn't be a decision based on anything else but her illness.

It was bad enough *she* had to make decisions based on cancer. She wouldn't ask it of him, too.

She couldn't.

A flash of white chiffon rushing past her knees startled her from her thoughts, and she quickly dodged the little flower girl, who was spinning around like the fairy princess she no doubt felt like on the dance floor. When the little girl turned, Hope caught a glimpse of the smile of sheer delight on her face. A moment later, her mother grabbed her hands and started dancing with her, and Hope was completely lost.

A little girl. Would she ever have a little girl?

A child of her own?

She looked back at Levi. There had been a time when she'd dreamed of having that with him. But they'd been kids then. It was a lifetime ago and so much had changed.

He was a traveler. He didn't want children. *"Not for a while."* Those had been his exact words when they'd casually discussed it after making love. At the time, it hadn't meant anything to Hope. Why would it? It was just casual conversation. And really, she hadn't considered the possibility of children for a few years beyond the vague concept of *one day*.

Things changed.

But what if they didn't have *awhile?*

Or more specifically, what if *she* didn't have awhile?

In that moment, her choice was made, and Hope knew without a doubt what she had to do.

She also knew that breaking up with him would be the hardest thing she ever had to do. Definitely harder than the first time they'd broken up. Because this time, she knew better.

She knew what it would mean, and she knew there would be no third chance at their love.

Hope also knew that it was exactly what she had to do.

Before she could chicken out, Hope took Levi by both hands and squeezed. "I need you to know how much I care about you."

"Of course, I—"

"No." She stopped him. "I need to say this, Levi. Please." Hope worked hard to swallow back the tears that threatened to overtake her. But she couldn't cry. If she started, she wasn't going to stop and then she'd never be able to say what she needed to. "I can't see you anymore. This was a mistake." The words tumbled out before she could change her mind. "I'm sorry if I led you on in anyway, but I..." She dropped her gaze for a moment, steeling herself. "It was just a big mistake," she said again, this time as she looked straight into his eyes. "I'm sorry."

Hope pulled her hands out of his and turned to walk away, when his voice stopped her. "Don't do this."

She froze for a minute, and looked back at him, careful to keep her face a cold mask of indifference that she didn't feel. "I need you to leave, Levi. We're in the middle of an event."

Hope saw the hurt in his eyes, the confusion followed by pain and it killed her, but she couldn't go back on what she'd just said. It was for his own good. He deserved the life that he wanted to live, not the one he felt he *had* to because of her illness. He'd thank her one day. "Please, Levi."

He opened his mouth to say something, but then glanced around at the festivities taking place all around him and closed it again. Without a word, Levi turned and walked away.

Hope's hand flew to her mouth in an attempt to muffle the cry that had escaped. She wanted to call him back. And she might have, too, but Faith appeared by her side. "What just happened?" She didn't give Hope a chance to answer. "Did you and Levi just... Hope, are you...oh shit."

Her sister wrapped her arm around her and led her as discreetly as she could off the dance floor and into the kitchen where finally, Hope let herself cry.

Chapter Eleven

"I DON'T GET IT." Levi felt like a broken record, but if Logan noticed, or even if he did, he didn't say a word. In fact, to his cousin's credit, he was being the perfect friend, letting Levi wallow in his sadness and broken-heartedness. It had been three days since Hope had broken up with him. Three days that Levi had tried to call her and text her and even stop by the ranch. Three days that he'd been met with total silence and avoidance. Which meant it had been three days that Levi had to feel even worse about what had happened.

"Why would she do that?" he continued. "Things were going so well."

"Were they?"

Levi shot his cousin a look.

"Yes," he confirmed. "*Very* well."

They'd been sitting in the Knot for the last hour and the only topic of conversation had been Hope. Or, more specifically, the way Hope had broken up with him and what possible reason she could have had for doing it.

"It was just over a week ago that we were at the house for

dinner, remember?" Logan nodded. "And then we went back to…well, I took her…"

"I get it," Logan said. "You took her home and *made love.* You told me a dozen times already." Logan lifted his beer and took a deep drink. "It was beautiful and magical and—"

Levi shot him a look that shut him up.

"Sorry," Logan mumbled. "But all I'm saying is that maybe it wasn't going as well as you thought it was, is all. I mean, obviously it wasn't because if it was, we wouldn't be sitting here right now, would we?"

He had a point, even if Levi didn't want to admit it.

"Maybe you're right." Levi drank deeply from his own glass before refilling it with the jug in front of them. "Maybe I misread everything."

But he *knew* he hadn't misread anything. The night they'd spent together *had* been amazing. And it wasn't just the sex— which was pretty friggin' fantastic—it was everything. It was the way they'd talked. *Really* talked. About the past. How the last few years had been for him on the fishing boats. The challenges, the dreams he'd had, the places he'd traveled. And for her, they'd talked out how hard things had been when her parents had died, and the challenges she'd faced getting Ever After Ranch off the ground. They'd held each other and talked about their dreams for the future. Dreams, he didn't want to admit at the time, that most definitely included her. Even when she'd mentioned children, he hadn't changed the subject like he once might have. Because the truth was, the idea of children didn't scare the hell out of him the way it used to. So he'd told her the truth.

He did want kids. But not for a while.

What he hadn't told her was that she was the only person in the world that he could ever actually imagine having children with. But not before he showed her the world. Because now that he had her back in his life and in his arms, he never wanted to let go. And more than anything, he wanted to give her the world. Literally. There'd be time for children later. After they'd traveled together. When Hope told him that she'd never traveled farther than Las Vegas once for a trip with her sister, Levi had made it his mission to take her places. To show her that as amazing as their hometown was, there was a whole world out there that was amazing, too.

Which was why he'd bought her the tickets to Mexico. The same tickets that had sparked everything to change.

Levi pulled the ticket confirmation from his pocket and slapped them onto the table between him and Logan. "I thought that's what she wanted," he said with a shake of his head. "She told me that she wanted to travel. But when I told her about the tickets, she..."

"Dumped you?"

Levi's head shot up and he once again glared at his cousin.

"Sorry," Logan added quickly. "But it's true, right? Maybe she didn't want to go to Mexico."

Levi shook his head and ran his hands through his hair. Beer wasn't helping to clear his head and talking to Logan *really* wasn't helping. He stared out the window at the street outside. "There has to be something else," he muttered under his breath. "None of it makes sense. And why is Faith here?" He'd almost forgotten that Hope's twin sister had been at the wedding, too. He'd been so preoccupied with everything else, but maybe it was all connected.

"Faith?" Logan sat straighter on his stool. "Faith is here?"

Levi looked at him sideways. "Why do you sound so interested?"

"I'm not." His cousin tried and failed to look casual about it, but they both knew there was only one reason why Logan sounded so interested in Faith. It was because he *was* interested. "It's just unusual is all."

"It *is* unusual." Levi watched his cousin carefully. As much as Logan tried to appear casual, Levi could tell he was anything but. "She was at the event on the weekend," he continued. "She was helping Hope."

"Helping Hope? I thought that's what you were supposed to do?"

Levi nodded. "I am." He shook his head. "I was. I...I don't actually know. Hope said something about how I wasn't going to stay and—"

"Are you not going to stay?"

Levi waved the question away. He'd turned down the offer from his boss to captain his own boat. It was a huge opportunity, but as of a few days ago, it didn't matter how big the opportunity was—it wasn't Hope. Now...*no!* It still wasn't Hope.

"Anyway," Levi continued. "She said she needed someone long term and that's why—"

"Faith is here long term?"

Again, Logan looked a little *too* interested.

Which was strange, because Faith and Logan had never actually dated. In fact, all he'd ever done was work to piss her off. When they were younger, Logan never failed to miss an opportunity to give Faith a hard time. A *really* hard time. He would tease her, and harass anyone she dated, even guys who didn't actually date her. It was as though he'd made it his personal mission to piss her off and get in her way of...well, anything. She used to hate hanging out with him when Hope and Levi insisted that they all do something together. Not that they suggested it very often because Logan and Faith and their obvious contempt for each other made any social situation way more awkward than it was worth.

"I have no idea, Logan. Remember how Hope won't talk to me? So I didn't really get around to asking her."

"Sorry," he mumbled and looked down into his drink.

Levi shook his head and once again looked out into the

street and the sunny day that was in direct contrast to how he felt at that moment. He watched the people on the sidewalk, carrying on as if the world hadn't just completely crumbled, when a flash of blonde on the other side of the street caught his eye.

Hope.

"I gotta go." Levi jumped up from his stool, tossed some money onto the table to cover his bill, and was out on the street before Logan could protest.

"Hope!" He yelled across the street as he narrowly missed a car from hitting him. "Wait. I—"

Hope turned around, and that's when he saw.

"Faith."

She nodded. "It's me. Sorry." She actually did look sorry for the mix-up. "It's nice to see you, Levi." She held out her arms and Levi gave her a quick hug. It never failed to hit him just how different the sisters were. Not many people could tell them apart so easily—and clearly he was a bit rusty with it— but they really were different.

"It's nice to see you, too, Faith." He took a step back. "But I'm not going to lie, I was—"

"Looking for Hope."

It wasn't a question, but he nodded in response just the same before looking past Faith's shoulder.

"She's not here," Faith said. "She's actually in the city today and—"

"Again?" An icy trail of concern worked its way up his spine. "She's sure going to the city a lot these days. What's going on?"

Faith looked as though she wanted to say something, but instead she just shrugged. It was a bullshit response and they both knew it.

"Talk to me, Faith. Please?"

She shook her head. "I can't. I'm sorry, Levi. But you really should talk to my sister."

"She won't talk to me!" He was vaguely aware that his voice was getting louder and a handful of people had turned to look at them, but he didn't care. "I've tried," he continued. "She's ignoring my calls and my texts, and I went by the ranch thinking I could talk to her and maybe even…oh, I don't know…do my job. But no one was there."

"Yeah." Faith shifted her tote higher on her shoulder. "It's been a bit strange around there. The wedding that was scheduled for this weekend canceled, something about an affair. I don't know, but it sounded messy. And we actually went ahead and canceled the event for next weekend. So there's—"

"Canceled?" Hope didn't cancel events. She'd made it super clear to him that she'd never cancel anything, especially a wedding. It wasn't fair to the couple. There was definitely something wrong. "What's going on?" he asked again. This time he wasn't going to let her brush him off.

Faith shifted from side to side, clearly uncomfortable saying anything, but at the same time, it looked as if that was exactly what she wanted to do. "Look, Levi." She grabbed his arm and pulled him to the side, away from the people trying to walk past. "I'm really sorry about the way my sister handled things," she said. "I really am. And just for the record, I don't agree with what she did at all."

"Well, that's—"

"But it's not my decision." She cut him off and held up a finger.

Levi's stomach sank. He'd let himself believe even for a second that he might have an ally.

"But just because it's not my decision doesn't mean I don't get my say." Hesitantly, he waited for the rest of what she was going to say. "And I think you deserve the truth. Even if it doesn't change Hope's mind, I believe she owes you that." He nodded. "So, come by the ranch tonight. About eight o'clock, okay?"

Levi had no idea how it would play out or how Faith was going to arrange anything, but he didn't care. It was an opening, and as small as it was, he'd take it.

"Thank you."

Faith offered him a sad smile and shook her head. "Don't thank me yet."

It had been a long day, but Hope was glad she'd decided to make the trip into the city in one day. She'd made the three-hour drive early, arriving at the doctor's office for nine thirty, and after going through her treatment plan and options for trying to conceive, she jumped back in the car and started the long drive home.

She'd gone back and forth over it, but in the end, she was glad she'd gone alone, despite Faith's insistence that she didn't mind accompanying her. She needed the time to think, and that's exactly what she did.

It had been days already since she'd broken up with Levi, and it still felt just as raw as it had the moment it happened. But now, along with the pain and sense of loss that had been overwhelming her, was something else.

Excitement.

After leaving Doctor Barrett's office with not only the prescription for the hormones that were supposed to delay the spread of the cancer long enough for her to have a child, and the literature on sperm donors, Hope could honestly say that the cloud that had hung over her for the last few days was starting to lift. Not a lot, but just a little bit. Because now, instead of focusing on what she'd lost, she could focus on what was in front of her.

Motherhood.

The very idea of it made her giddy.

She'd always known that one day she wanted to have a child. *One day.* But beyond an abstract thought, it had never been more than that. Now, it was real.

She pulled into the yard in front of the house and gathered up the stack of papers on the passenger seat with a smile on her face. Once she read through the information, Doctor Barrett said she could make the appointment with the donor clinic whenever she was ready—the sooner the better—and get started.

Feasibly, in a few months she could be pregnant.

The idea stopped her in her tracks before she reached for the door handle. As exciting as it was to think about being a mother, it was also terrifying. Because in all of her abstract thoughts about having a baby over the years, none of those thoughts had involved her doing it on her own.

Not once.

In fact, there had been a few times when Levi had factored into those thoughts.

No. If she was honest, it had definitely been more than a few times.

Sadness washed over her again as she walked into the house. But as soon as the melancholy feeling came, she forced herself to push it from her mind. Levi didn't want a baby. He wanted to travel and see the world. That was a lifestyle that most certainly didn't lend itself to being a family man. And there was no way she would make him choose. It wasn't his cancer diagnosis to live with. And it wasn't as if they'd been together for years or were married, or...no. It wasn't right even to ask.

She just had to forget that she had ever let herself consider that Levi could be part of her future. Besides, it's not as though she had time to feel sorry for herself. And even if she did, it wouldn't be good for the baby.

The baby.

And she *was* going to have a baby. The thought put a smile right back on her face.

"What are you grinning about?" Faith's voice snapped her from her thoughts. "I didn't think a trip to your cancer doctor would make you happy."

Hope couldn't help but laugh as she walked past her sister into the kitchen, slapping the handful of papers and pamphlets into her hands as she went. "Check it out."

Faith was right behind her. "These are papers about sperm donors." Hope turned to see Faith staring at her quizzically. "So you've made your decision? I thought you were still thinking."

She couldn't look at Faith in the eye, not when she had that look on her face. That look that was full of concern and disapproval. She knew her sister wanted her to just have the hysterectomy and be done with it. And there was a large part of her that had considered it. After all, it was the best chance she had at beating the cancer. It gave her the highest odds. But…she couldn't ignore the pull of having her own child. She just couldn't. No matter what it might cost her.

"I guess I did." Hope hoped she sounded casual. She peeked into the oven. Faith wasn't much of a cook, but she was good at picking up food to warm up and serve, and as far as Hope was concerned, that was good enough. "Smells good."

"It's just a rotisserie chicken," Faith said absentmindedly. "Are we going to talk about this?" She waved the papers in the air and Hope sank into a kitchen chair with a sigh.

"What's to talk about?"

"Your life, Hope. That's what there is to talk about."

"I'm not dying."

"You could!" Faith struggled to control her emotions, and Hope had to look away. "If you don't get the surgery, Hope…" Her voice fell. "You could die. And I can't…"

Guilt flooded her as she listened to her twin sister try and fail to control her emotions, but Hope couldn't let herself even consider an alternative. She'd made her decision. She couldn't go back. Hope sat at the table and stared at her fingers and waited her sister out while she wiped at her eyes, trying desperately not to cry. Hope knew Faith well and she knew how much it pissed her off when she cried. Faith hated to show too much emotion.

Finally, Faith pulled herself together. "So that's it then?"

Hope nodded.

"And that's why you broke up with Levi?"

The question probably should have startled her, but it didn't. Part of her had been expecting it and wondering what had taken Faith so long. She answered honestly. "Yes."

Faith shook her head and mumbled something Hope couldn't quite make out. She didn't bother asking for clarification.

"That's probably the stupidest thing I've ever heard," Faith said after a second. "I mean, stupider only to the fact that you're doing this in the first place."

"Faith…"

Her sister held up her hands. "I know, I know. It's your decision, but you're my twin sister, which means I'm still allowed to have an opinion." Hope wasn't sure that's what it meant at all, but she kept her mouth closed. "And I think it's important that you know what mine is."

"Noted."

"Okay," Faith said. "But I have one more thing to say."

"I'm sure you do."

"I think it was a shitty thing you did."

Hope was genuinely taken aback. "Shitty? What was shitty?"

"What you did to Levi." Faith pushed up from the table and stood. "It was a shitty thing to do."

"No. It wasn't." Hope shook her head. "I did it *for* him, Faith." She could feel the emotions she'd been carefully pushing down start to bubble up to the surface.

"He deserves to know the truth, Hope."

"No." She shook her head and looked down at the table.

"You need to give him more credit," Faith said. "He can handle it."

"No, I—"

"I can, you know."

Hope jumped at the sound of his voice and spun in her chair to see Levi in the doorway. *How much had he heard?* Enough, obviously.

Dammit.

"Levi."

"What's going on, Hope?" He crossed the room, took her hands in his, and dropped to his knees in front of her chair. "Talk to me."

She shook her head and glanced to her sister, who only gave her a knowing look and nodded curtly before walking out of the room and leaving them alone.

She could kill her sister, but part of her knew she was right. And that was the part that pissed her off the most. Hope looked back at Levi, and steeled herself against the look of concern and—love—in his eyes.

Double dammit.

She closed her eyes for a second, took a deep breath and decided to just rip the Band-Aid off. "I have cancer." It was the first time she'd said the word aloud and it took her off guard for a moment. "It's not a terribly big deal," she added quickly. "The doctor said we caught it early, but I've made a decision to have a baby before I get the surgery and I decided not to tell you because it wouldn't be fair to you but I couldn't stay with you either because that's really not fair and Faith doesn't agree with my choice and thinks I'm being stupid but it doesn't matter what Faith thinks because it's not her body and it's not her life and I've made my decision and it's final and I'm sorry if I hurt you in any way, but I need to be true to myself."

She finished in a rush and closed her eyes again, unable to look at Levi and his reaction.

It took a minute, but finally, Levi spoke. "Are you done?"

She nodded before opening her eyes.

"You have cancer?"

She nodded again.

"And you're having a baby?"

She nodded and then shrugged and nodded again.

"And that's your final decision?"

This time she spoke. "It is. And I meant what I said, Levi. It's my final decision."

"Okay."

"I'm not—okay?" Hope stopped and looked at him curiously.

"Of course it's okay," he said. "I'm not going to try to influence your decision, Hope. I mean, I obviously don't understand everything since I just found out about it, and I'm still trying to wrap my head around the whole *cancer* thing, but you're a smart woman and you don't need me to tell you what to do with your body."

She hadn't expected that from him. Hope sat up a little straighter and blew out a breath she hadn't realized she'd been holding. His support helped, but it didn't change her other decision.

"Did you really think I'd try to change your mind? Is that why you pushed me away?"

It broke her heart to look in his eyes, but Faith was right; he deserved the truth. "I pushed you away, Levi, because I'm having a child on my own." She pulled her hands out of his and tucked them into her lap. "This is my decision and mine alone. I'm not going to involve anyone else. And I'm not going to let anyone change my mind either."

Levi got to his feet and took a step back from her, which gave Hope the chance to stand and move across the room from him. She needed space.

"Hope, this doesn't make any—"

"No." She held her hand up to stop him. "I won't change my mind, Levi. I can't."

"But, Hope, that's—"

"No." She shook her head and looked at her feet. "I need you to go. This is all hard enough."

She refused to look up. She refused to meet his eyes because she knew exactly what she would see there and she knew it would break her resolve. "Please," she said quietly. "Just go." Hope waited until she could hear his footsteps and then finally the closing of the door as he left.

It was only then that she let the tears she was only barely holding back slide down her face. She didn't know whether she'd made the right decision or not. But she knew if she'd let him, Levi would have declared his loyalty to her, despite whatever it was he dreamed of doing. He would put his whole life on hold for her, and as much as she wanted him by her side, she would never be able to look at him and not feel bad for what he'd chosen because of her.

She wasn't sure how long she stood there, letting the sadness fill her, threatening to break her. But finally, when her sister pulled her into a hug, she didn't resist, but let herself melt into Faith's embrace and cry.

Chapter Twelve

FAITH SHOULD HAVE BEEN THRILLED that they had two whole weeks without any weddings to worry about. And she might have been if she wasn't so worried about her sister. Hope had hardly left her room in the two days since Levi had come over and more or less ambushed her in the kitchen, demanding answers. And yes, Faith did feel a little bad about that, but not really. Hope owed him the truth. And even if it had broken his heart, it was probably for the best that he knew what was really going on.

Faith had also secretly hoped that it would make Hope feel better or at least talking to Levi directly to his face would make her change her mind on...well, everything. But she'd underestimated her sister's stubbornness.

And of course, Hope's falling out with Levi also meant that he was no longer helping out at the ranch. As far as Faith was concerned, that might be the biggest problem with her sister's decision. At least in the short term, because Hope had decided that a reprieve in hosting actual weddings was a good opportunity for Faith to take inventory of everything they had in the storage shed.

It was a job that she was absolutely positive wouldn't have been assigned if Levi were around. Or even if it was, at least he'd be there to help her out. As it was, the assignment was definitely not helping her feel any better about the entire wedding business. Quite the opposite. The sheer quantity of supplies that Hope had acquired was insane. Even more mind-boggling was the apparent organizational system that her sister had. Which, from what Faith could tell, wasn't really much of a system at all.

She stood with her hands on her hips, staring at the shelves where the chair covers were held, and shook her head. There appeared to be about ten different shades of blue in there. With a deep sigh, Faith reached for one and tugged, pulling it free from the stack, only narrowly avoiding the rest of the fabric from tumbling down.

"Now, is this royal blue or peacock blue?" She held the material at arm's length before tossing it to the side and reaching for another one. This time she didn't have the same luck, and the entire shelf of blue chair covers toppled down at her.

Faith muttered a string of curses as she extracted herself from the sea of blue that covered her feet. "Screw this." She turned and walked away from the mess and out the door of the storage shed into the spring sunshine.

It was way too beautiful of a day to be spent inside that dingy little shed anyway.

And that's exactly what she'd tell her sister—if she asked. Faith glanced toward the house as she made her way to Hope's SUV parked in the yard. The curtains to her sister's room were still closed. No doubt she was still up there, poring over the artificial insemination information in an effort to convince herself that she was doing the right thing. Either way, Hope wasn't likely to notice if Faith took off.

Besides, it's not like she was her boss.

Well, not really anyway.

Faith found a parking spot just off Main Street and was just putting the vehicle in park when her cell phone chirped with an incoming message.

Talk to me, Faith. I miss you.

Faith shook her head and pressed her lips together.

Noah had texted her almost every day since she'd left. The messages had all been different. Some long, telling her about things at the office, and the cases she used to be assigned to. Some short, with just an emoji or little message. And then there'd been ones more like this one. With a short, but pointed message.

She hadn't replied to any of them.

Faith stuck her phone into her purse and slipped from the vehicle. She knew she was being cowardly, and she knew that Noah deserved better from her. But the problem was, she didn't know what exactly it was that Noah deserved from her. She'd been honest from the beginning. She didn't *do* relationships. She never wanted one with him. Not with anyone. It wasn't her fault he'd gotten attached. It wasn't her fault that he'd ignored everything she'd said and tried to make her into something she wasn't. She couldn't be responsible for that. Because the truth was, she'd never misled Noah. She'd always known that it was only one thing she wanted from him.

Liar.

Faith pulled her purse higher on her shoulder and wound her way through the parking lot to the front of the hardware store, pushing the little voice in the back of her head down. She didn't have time to think about how Noah may or may not be handling her absence. She had her sister to worry about. And like it or not, she also had Ever After Ranch to worry about. And that needed to be her priority.

She worked her way through the aisles of the hardware store, collecting the items she'd been looking for. Faith had no idea how long she would be working with Hope at the ranch, but something told her it was going to be longer than she'd originally expected. And if that was the case, she was going to change a few things. At least the things that were going to help her stay organized.

Equipped with a stack of large plastic totes all with colored lids and a label maker, fifteen minutes later, Faith pushed her way outside, balancing the totes in front of her. A little too late, she realized she probably should have taken the cart because she couldn't see anything, but it seemed like more work to go back into the store than to just manage and get back to the car.

Of course, that was easier said than done when a moment later, Faith ran smack into something—or as it turned out, someone—and her carefully balanced stack of totes tumbled to the ground.

"Shit." She instantly dropped to her knees to try to collect her things. "Are you okay?" She threw the question over her shoulder without looking up.

"Still falling for me, are you, Turner?"

The voice cut through her. Her things forgotten, Faith jumped to her feet to look directly into the familiar deep-brown eyes. "Logan."

"Miss me?"

"Not even a little."

His smile was still every bit as cocky as it had been when they were young. Maybe more so. And something about the way he looked at her made her stomach flip, but just a little and only until he spoke again. "Oh, come on," he teased. "You don't have to lie to me."

She scoffed and shook her head. "You wish, Logan. Every moment that I've been away from here—and you—has been blissful."

For a moment, she could have sworn his tough exterior cracked a little and there was a flicker of disappointment in his eyes, which was ridiculous because they'd only ever gotten under each other's skin. But then it was gone and his smile was back to full power, leaving Faith to imagine that she'd seen it at all.

"Let me help you with that." He bent and started collecting the totes and lids before she could object.

"I've got it." Faith tried to take a lid from his hand, but he held fast. "Logan! I said, I've—"

She tugged as she spoke and when Logan released his grip, she toppled backward, landing hard on her ass on the sidewalk. "Got it," she finished lamely.

"Faith, I'm sorry." Logan stood over her, a genuine look of apology on his face as he offered her his hand. "Are you—"

"I'm fine, Logan." She pushed past his hand and got to her feet. "I don't need your help." Her words came out even more harshly than she'd intended and immediately she felt badly. That was, until he spoke again.

"You never did, did you, Faith."

His words bit through her, but he'd turned to walk away before she could retaliate.

"What does that even mean?" she called after him but he didn't turn around. "Logan!" she yelled, hating herself even as she did it. "What does that mean?"

If Levi spent any more time sulking around the house, his aunt was going to sit him down with a big bowl of her homemade soup and not let him up until he'd confessed everything. And if she didn't get to him, Katie would get there first.

The problem was, Levi didn't know what he would confess to. Or what he'd even say.

Hope had cancer.
Hope wanted to have a baby.
Hope didn't want his baby.

He had no idea where to start or what to say, or hell, even what to feel.

After he'd left her house two nights earlier, he'd gotten in his truck and driven in a state of shock. It was over ten minutes and many miles before he noticed he'd missed the turn to the Langdon ranch. Uncaring, he'd pulled to the edge of the logging road and scrambled down the bank to the river below. The water soothed him. It always had. When he'd been a kid, it had been the creeks, streams, and rivers that he'd be drawn to. As well as the lake down the highway, of course, but only when it wasn't full of tourists or boatloads of people partying. It was the solitude he craved. The sound of the water, and the ability to think and let his mind grow still.

It's what drew him to the coast and ultimately the fishing boats where he'd spent his years. The work was hard. Very hard. Even after a lifetime mostly growing up on a ranch, Levi hadn't been fully prepared for how physically challenging the work would be. For days, every muscle in his body ached and protested against the work. He might have quit, too, like so many of the new recruits did, but Levi found he actually liked the strain on his muscles. The aches and pains reminded him that he was alive when every other part of him felt lost and dead to the life he'd had back on the ranch.

And then there was the lure of the sea. When everything else was lost—his dreams, his love, the ranch, his cousins, his aunt, and the life he'd had—he had the roll of the ocean beneath his feet, the smell of the salty air, and the gentle lap of the waves as they washed up on the dock when they were in port. Those years had cleared his head in a way that he'd never expected. In that time away, he'd gained perspective, grown up, learned a lot. Mostly about himself. But the world, too.

But all of the learning and growing he'd done could never have prepared him for the heartache that ripped through his body now. Never in his life, not when he'd left Glacier Falls and

Hope behind the first time, not when he'd watched a crew member succumb to his injuries after a terrible fishing accident, and not even when his mother had died when he was only a boy had Levi experienced the type of full body pain that could only be caused by a broken heart.

The type of pain he was experiencing now and, for the first time, being near the water didn't calm him. It didn't soothe him or clear his head or relieve any of the pressure that was building in his head. It made it worse.

Which was why he'd spent the last few days shuffling between his bed and the couch. And also why his auntie and cousin were about ready to drag him into reality whether he liked it or not.

"Levi? Are you in there?" Katie was home.

Levi pulled his pillow over his head. It had only been a matter of time before they'd had enough of him. Katie and Auntie Deb were never ones to let any of them wallow in their own misery. Still, he'd hoped they'd take a little bit of pity on him. But no such luck, because a moment later, there was a knock on the door.

Before he could call out some excuse that he was naked—a warning he was pretty sure she wouldn't heed anyway—his cell phone rang. Levi lunged for it on the nightstand and held it up triumphantly. "I have to take this call!" he hollered to his cousin through the door before pushing the button and answering it—all without looking at the caller.

"Hello." He tried and failed to instill any enthusiasm into his voice. "Levi Langdon."

"Levi? Is that you?" His captain's crusty voice, salty from the sea and too many cigars, crackled over the line.

Shit.

He really should have looked at the caller ID. He'd been avoiding Captain Pat ever since he sent the email back that he wasn't interested in the job offer. A decision that, given Hope's subsequent behavior, he wasn't sure was the right one. The calls and texts—which were unusual because Levi didn't even think that Captain Pat *knew* how to text—had been almost nonstop ever since.

"It's me, Captain Pat."

"So you're not dead?"

"No." *Although I might as well be.* "I'm not dead. Sorry, I just—"

"I don't want to listen to your excuses." The captain cut him off smoothly. "I'm a busy man. And frankly, I don't care. I need an answer, Langdon. Do you want your own boat, or not?"

Levi squeezed his eyes shut for a moment. His own boat. *What would that mean?*

It would mean more money, more opportunity. His own crew. Doing things his way. It would mean realizing the dream he'd held onto for years, ever since he finished out his first season on a boat.

But it would also mean moving back to the coast. This time for good.

There was a time, not so long ago, that he would have jumped at that opportunity. But now...now that Hope...

What? Now that Hope had pushed him away? Rejected him for good? Found out she was sick and possibly could die and...

"Langdon? I'm waiting." Captain Pat's voice cut through his thoughts.

Fuck.

No matter what Hope said, no matter how hard she pushed, Levi knew the truth. He sat up so quickly, pillows tumbled to the floor as he swung his legs over the edge of his bed. He did know the truth. And Hope knew it, too; she just needed to be reminded. "Sorry, Captain," he said clearly into the phone. "I want to thank you for the opportunity because it is a good one."

"Damn right it is."

"But my answer stands. I have to turn it down."

"You have to *what?*"

Levi shook his head, but he couldn't help the smile that crossed his face as everything finally became clear. "I have to turn it down, Captain, because I don't think I'll be returning to the coast for a while. I have important things to take care of here."

Very important things.

"Important things, huh?" The captain huffed. "Sounds like a woman to me."

"Not just any woman," Levi said confidently, never more sure that he'd made the right choice. "But the only woman I've ever loved." He ran a hand over his face and almost laughed at the scruff he'd acquired over the last few days of feeling sorry for himself. "She needs me, Captain. And I need her. More than I ever realized."

On the other end of the line, the gruff captain made a noise that sounded somewhere between a cough and a grunt. No doubt, Captain Pat had never heard such soft-hearted sentiment from any of his crew before, but Levi didn't care.

"Langdon, I've spent many years at sea," Captain Pat started. "Not all of them have been good years." He continued in the slow, precise way he had. "Some of them have been great years." Levi nodded and waited. "But even the best year at sea could never match the worst year with a good woman."

Whatever Levi had thought Captain Pat was going to say, it wasn't that. He swallowed hard and was thankful the older man wasn't there to see the look of shock on his face.

"Oh, go on and close your mouth, Langdon," the captain said, as if reading his thoughts. "It's not like I've lived the life of a monk, you know? There was a woman in my life once, too. My biggest love and my biggest regret. Don't make that same mistake, Langdon."

"No sir."

"You do what you need to do," Captain Pat continued. "And if you ever find yourself on the coast in need of a job, there'll always be a boat for you."

Levi shook his head and grinned. "Thank you, Captain. You don't know what that means to me." But the captain had already hung up.

Levi tucked his phone in his back pocket and sprinted across the room with a newfound energy. Now that everything had become clear and the decision had been made, he didn't want to waste one more minute. He'd already wasted enough time allowing himself to feel sorry for himself instead of fighting for what he wanted—and needed.

He flung open the door to see Katie on the other side, a pointed look on her normally sweet face. "If you think you're going to her like that, you have another think coming." She sniffed the air in disgust. "Seriously, when was the last time you had a shower?"

Levi couldn't help it; he laughed. "Did you just hear that?" He gestured behind him as if he'd had the conversation with the captain right there in the bedroom.

"I did," Katie said. "Not that I needed to overhear anything to know that you're desperately in love with Hope Turner. We've all known that for years. We were just waiting for you to realize it too."

Levi stared at his cousin.

"What?" she said in defense. "We did. And you did, too. Frankly, I'm a little disappointed that you needed to wallow for a few days like a heart-sick teenage boy before a conversation with an old man helped change your mind." Katie crossed her arms. "I thought you were smarter than that."

Levi smacked her arm playfully. "You knew? And you let me behave like an ass just because?"

Katie laughed. "Not just because. But because you needed

to come to it yourself, Levi. You're a grown-ass man. You don't need me telling you what you already know. Do you?"

"No." He shook his head with a smile. "I needed to work through it on my own."

"But seriously, what is your plan? Are you really going to just storm over to the ranch looking like a scrub who doesn't know what a razor is and declare your love for her? Because I think you can do better, Levi. And really…" She raised her eyebrows as she looked him over. "You totally *should* do better."

Her words stopped him. She was right. This was the woman he loved more than life itself, and not only did he need to convince her of that, he needed to make sure she knew without a doubt that he was not going anywhere. No matter what life threw at them, he wanted to be at her side for all of it. The good and the bad. No matter what.

"You're right," he said as an idea formulated. "I need something amazing." A smile spread across his face so wide that Katie laughed and shook her head.

"What are you thinking? Because you look either very excited or a little manic."

Levi grabbed his cousin's hand and pulled her toward the kitchen. "I have an idea," he said. "But I'm going to need your help." He stopped suddenly and stared at her. "Actually, I'm going to need a lot of help. We need to call Faith."

Chapter Thirteen

HOPE WAS DONE FEELING sorry for herself. At least she was going to pretend she was. *Fake it till you make it, right?*

She'd given herself a day to wallow in her misery, but that was it. After all, it was her decision to push Levi away. She'd made a choice and now she had to live with it. Besides, even if she wanted to feel sorry for herself, she didn't have time. She had plans to make. Her life was about to change in a huge way, and the best way to get over a heartbreak was to throw yourself in a new project.

Which was exactly what she was doing by cleaning out the bedroom next to hers so she could turn it into a nursery. The idea had come to her in the middle of the night. It might be a little bit presumptuous to assume that she wasn't going to have any trouble getting pregnant, and maybe some might consider it bad luck, but Hope didn't care. The idea that in less than a year from now she could be holding her very own baby in her arms made her heart ache with an intense want.

And considering there was nothing she could do at that moment to speed up the process of actually getting pregnant, the next best thing was to create the perfect space for her future baby. Which was easier said than done, considering the spare room had been used as a storage space for the last few years because Hope had been too busy to take things up to the attic properly, or get rid of them altogether.

She lost herself in the task of sorting through the old things, making piles of things to donate, throw away, or take up to the attic for storage. Hope didn't know how long she'd been working before she heard the sound of the front door slam, followed by Faith's voice calling out for her.

"I'm up here," she yelled from behind a pile of her dad's old books. "In the spare room."

A moment later, Faith popped her head inside. "What are you doing in here?"

"Cleaning." Hope waved her arms around and laughed a little. Whatever she was doing, it certainly didn't look as if she'd actually cleaned anything. "Well, organizing anyway. I thought I'd turn this room into the baby's room."

Faith's smile dipped a little bit at the mention of the baby. Hope knew her sister wasn't happy with her decision, and she couldn't blame her, not really. Faith was only looking out for her best interests, but what she didn't understand was that a baby *was* in her best interest. She felt it deep down; she was going to be fine. The cancer was in the early stages and the doctor said so as well. She had time. But this would be the only time. Hope knew her sister would change her mind about all of it as soon as she saw her new niece or nephew. She'd fall in love with the baby, too. There was no doubt.

"What are you up to?" Hope changed the subject as she stacked another book. "I'm sorry that I've been kind of absent from the barn for the last few days. I just…well…"

"It's okay." Faith shrugged. "I've been taking inventory like you suggested." A sly smile crept over her sister's face. "And reorganizing a little."

"What?" Hope shook her head and sighed. She and Faith had very different ideas on how to organize and no doubt her type-A sister had created a sterile and structured system that wouldn't make any sense to Hope. She'd just have to fix it later. "Whatever," she said, deciding not to pick a fight.

"But I'm actually here for you," Faith said. "I decided we needed a little fun around here and something to smile about."

Hope couldn't argue with that. She sat back and listened.

"So, I was thinking that we could do something that we used to."

"What's that?"

"Guess."

Hope shook her head with a laugh. "You're being ridiculous. I literally have no idea what you're talking about. What did we used to do? Like when we were kids?"

Faith nodded. "Little kids." She fed her another clue. "It was your favorite thing and you always begged me to do it, even after I thought it was stupid. In fact, I think this is the first time I've been here when you haven't asked—"

"Wedding sisters!" Hope jumped to her feet with excitement. She'd always loved playing wedding sisters with Faith, and she'd been so sad when Faith declared the whole idea of weddings and love stupid and refused to play with her anymore. It hadn't stopped her from secretly playing without her sister, but it was never the same. After all, you could hardly pretend to get married to someone if you were the only one playing. "Seriously? You *want* to play?"

Faith laughed. "No. Not at all. But *you* do, don't you?"

Hope nodded without hesitation. The timing was terrible, to be sure, but if Faith was really offering to "play" with her, there was no way she was going to say no. "I do," she said quickly. "I really do. Is that silly? I mean, we're grownups."

Faith laughed. "It *is* silly. Beyond silly. I mean, I thought it was completely ridiculous when we were kids, but..." She shrugged. "You are my sister, and I love you and I know things haven't been awesome lately and…well, I just want to see you smile. So if playing dress-up is going to make you smile, I'll do it."

Hope jumped over the pile of books and wrapped her sister up in a tight hug. "Thank you, Faith. Really. Thank you."

"Yeah, yeah." Faith wiggled out of her arms. "And I'm even going to let you be the bride."

"No," Hope objected. "You can be the bride. After all, I know you don't want to—"

"Look it. The only way I'm doing this is if I get to be the groom and that's final."

Not about to argue with her, Hope agreed to the terms, and together they went to get ready.

"What am I going to wear?" Hope stood in front of her closet. When they were little, and played the game, they would dress up in their Easter dresses, and an old veil that had been left behind from one of the weddings their parents had held ages ago at the ranch, long before it was Ever After Ranch. But Hope didn't have an Easter dress anymore. And nothing that even remotely looked bridal. "I guess I can wear the gray dress I bought for a Christmas party a few years ago."

"You are *not* wearing gray as a bride." Faith rolled her eyes. "I may not be all traditional, but if we're doing this, we're doing it right. Also, you wore a *gray* dress to a Christmas party? Really?"

Hope playfully smacked her sister's arm but Faith just laughed.

"Hold on." Faith disappeared into the hall and returned a moment later with a garment bag. "Here, wear this."

"What is that?"

"A dress." Faith gave her a look of exasperation.

"Right." Hope took it and laid it on the bed. "But where did you get it?"

Her sister looked away and shrugged. "I found it in the shed. It's no biggie."

"The shed?" Hope stared at her. There was *no* way she'd found a wedding dress in the shed.

"Someone must have left it there." Faith shrugged and unzipped the garment bag before pulling out a lacy, ivory dress.

As soon as Hope saw the dress, she forgot all about how it might have appeared in her shed because it was absolutely gorgeous.

She must have gasped a little as Faith lifted it and held it out to her because the smile on her sister's face matched Hope's reaction. She walked over to it slowly and ran her fingers down the bodice. It was a simple cut. A sweetheart neckline, fitted through the body with a flare just below the hips to give the skirt a little fullness. But not too much. It was classy and elegant and exactly the kind of dress she would have picked for herself.

"I don't know how you did this, Faith. But it's absolutely perfect."

Faith grinned and handed Hope the dress. "I know. Now get dressed."

"I don't know," Hope called from the bathroom. "Maybe this was a dumb idea. I feel stupid." Hope turned around and examined herself one more time in the mirror before cracking the door a little. "Faith? Did you hear me?"

"I heard you," her sister responded. "I'm just choosing to ignore you. Now hurry up."

Hope shook her head and looked again in the mirror. The wedding dress fit her perfectly. She'd tied her hair back in a simple knot, and put on a little makeup. She looked like a bride.

And maybe that was the whole problem. She looked like a bride, but she definitely wasn't one.

Which was the point of the game, she supposed. But now that she was all dressed up, the game no longer seemed as fun as it had when they were kids. Now, knowing she'd likely never *really* be a bride, the game suddenly felt sad and depressing.

"Maybe we shouldn't do this." Hope spoke into the mirror, no longer sure who exactly she was talking to. "Let's just get—"

"No." The bathroom door pushed open and Faith stood in the doorway, dressed in what could only be described as a rather sexy pantsuit with a very low-cut blouse beneath her jacket.

"What are you wearing?" Hope, momentarily distracted from her own reflection, took in her sister's take on *groom*.

"Just because I'm going to pretend to be the groom doesn't mean I can't look hot, too." She put her hand on her hip and winked, making Hope laugh. "But damn, girl. *You* look amazing." Faith slowly shook her head in awe as she took in her sister, making Hope feel self-conscious all over again. "It doesn't matter how smokin' the groom looks, does it? The bride will always steal the show." Faith laughed. "Seriously, you look stunning. Are you ready?" Before Hope could protest again, because she really was starting to think that trying to reenact a silly game from when they were kids was ludicrous, Faith grabbed her hand and pulled her from the bathroom.

"What else do we need?"

"Are we really doing this?"

Faith nodded. "I said we would, and we will. All of it. Music, flowers, dancing, the whole bit." Her sister crossed her arms and tried to look serious. "I'm a wedding planner now, you know? I have skills you haven't even seen yet."

Hope burst out laughing. "Oh, I believe it. I always knew you secretly loved the idea of all this."

The smile on her sister's face flickered and she looked away. "Here," she said without looking at Hope. "Put your shoes on and I'll get your veil sorted."

Hope did as directed. She knew she'd hit a nerve with Faith. It was the same nerve she'd hit since they were kids, but Faith would never tell her why she'd all of a sudden stopped playing the wedding game with her, and why she'd gone from a little girl just as obsessed with all things love and marriage as she'd been, to a hard, disillusioned teenager who had grown up into a woman with a chip on her shoulder who kept everyone at arm's length, seemingly overnight.

"Talk to me, Faith." It was time for answers. "What happened? Why do you hate all of this so much?"

"I don't hate it."

"That's a lie and you know it."

Faith offered her a small smile over her shoulder and shrugged before turning around again.

"Tell me, what happened?" Hope pushed. "Why do you work so hard to convince everyone that you don't care? Because I know you do. You must."

Faith's spine stiffened and she shook her head slightly.

"Faith?" Hope continued. "Why didn't you ever tell me? We told each other everything. What happened, Faith?" She knew she was pushing and she was very aware that there was a very real risk of pushing too far, of Faith blowing up and walking away just the way she always did. Hell, Faith had moved to the city the first chance she got, so she didn't have to face whatever it was that haunted her. But even with Faith's history of running, Hope needed to try again to know what was going on. The way she should have years ago.

Finally, her sister turned around. "Does it matter?" she asked softly. "It was so long ago."

Hope nodded. "Of course it does." She reached for Faith's hands. "You're my sister, and I love you."

A smile crossed Faith's face. "And I love you. Which is why I'm not going to ruin our wedding day with this kind of talk." She squeezed her hands in her own and laughed. "I promise there will be time to talk about all this later."

"You do?"

Faith looked straight in her eyes. "I do."

It was Hope's turn to laugh. "You *have* been practicing. I'm impressed."

"Don't get used to it. This is a one-shot deal." Faith affixed the veil to Hope's head and lifted it gently down over her face. "Now, let's go get this over with."

As far as plans went, Levi's was full of problems. Big ones.

There really were a million potential ways it could go wrong. Now that the wheels were in motion, he couldn't stop obsessing about each and every one of those potential pitfalls. The biggest one being that Hope wouldn't show up. What if, despite her certainty, Faith couldn't get her there?

Levi paced in the grass, keeping his eyes focused on his feet in an effort to calm himself down.

Faith would get her there. She knew her sister better than anyone. Even better than he did in many ways.

But what if she rejected his grand gesture once she got there?

He turned and paced in the opposite direction as he contemplated yet another pitfall.

"You need to stop that." Logan put his hand on Levi's shoulder in an attempt to stop his pacing.

"I can't."

"You have to, Levi." Something in Logan's voice made Levi pause. "She's here."

Levi spun around to see that Logan hadn't been lying.

She was there.

Hope was there. And she looked beautiful.

He had no idea how she'd pulled it off, but Faith had not only delivered her sister to him, but she was dressed as the most beautiful bride in the perfect spot. They'd pulled up in the golf cart that Hope used to whip around the property. She wasn't looking in his direction, but was instead saying something to her sister. Levi watched, and waited while Hope turned to step out of the cart and for the first time noticed what he'd set up.

Levi took a step toward her, and he saw the moment that Hope realized that whatever Faith had told her to get her there had been a lie. Her beautiful smile was gone, replaced by a frown. She shook her head and turned around, but Faith was right there to stop her if she thought she was going to leave. She took her arm and whispered something into her ear.

Hope nodded and looked down at her feet for a moment. When she looked up, she looked past the small crowd of people sitting in the chairs waiting for her; she looked past the beautiful arch he'd set up in her favorite place on the riverbank, and past the wildflowers that had been arranged by Katie in galvanized buckets down the aisle.

She looked past all of it and instead focused completely on him.

Levi smiled and moved quickly toward her, closing the distance between them in only a few strides. He noticed vaguely that Faith stepped back to give them privacy, but he only had eyes for the woman he loved.

"You look gorgeous."

"Levi? What's this all about?" Unshed tears shone in her eyes, but something else was there, too. Love.

Emboldened, he took her hands in his. "Hope, I love you. I always have."

She shook her head a little, but he wasn't deterred. "And I know you love me, too." She squeezed her eyes shut and a tear slipped down her cheek. "No." He brushed her tear away. "Don't cry. Because it's not a bad thing."

She looked up then, confusion in her eyes.

"It's not," he said again. "Love can never be a bad thing, Hope, and I know that you have some sort of crazy idea that we can't be together because you're sick."

"It's not that, Levi." She finally spoke. "I can't let you give up your life and everything you want because of me. I would never be able to live with myself if I knew that you gave up—"

"You?" He interrupted her. "You'd never be able to live with yourself if I gave *you* up?"

"No." She shook her head. "If you gave up everything you wanted out of life because I made the decision to do this...to have a...you don't understand."

He laughed a little then; he couldn't help it. "No," he said. "It's you who doesn't understand, Hope. Because the only thing I want out of my life is you." She blinked hard and tilted her head. "It's always been you, Hope." He squeezed her hands. "I love you, and I want to spend the rest of my life with you. Whatever it looks like."

"You have a whole life."

"I want you."

"But you want to travel."

He shook his head. "I want you."

"But you told me that you wanted to explore the world and—"

"I want *you*, Hope. Just you. We can figure out the rest of it later."

Tears flowed freely down her cheeks now. "But I want a baby, Levi, and that's not fair to ask you."

"Woman." He cupped her chin with one hand and gently tipped her head up so she looked into his eyes. "Do you really not understand what I'm saying here?" He grinned. "I love you and I want you and I want a life with you. All of it. If that means doing things a little out of order from what I thought about once, then who cares? None of that matters. The only thing that matters is you and me. I *love* you, Hope. I want to be with you. I want to share a life with you, and I want to have a baby with you."

A sob escaped her lips, and she pressed her free hand to her mouth.

"And," Levi continued, "since you mentioned it, what's not fair is that you didn't ask me what I wanted in any of this." He winked at her and she laughed.

It was a sweet sound that made Levi's heart clench in his chest.

Damn, but he loved her.

"I'm sorry." Her smile was the only apology he'd ever need. "I probably should have asked."

"Speaking of asking questions." Levi gave her a quick kiss on the cheek and dropped to one knee as he pulled a ring box from his suit pocket.

"Levi! What are—"

"Hope Turner," he started. "It should be no secret by now that I love you." He took a deep breath. "I've always loved you, and I will always love you. No matter what life throws at us, we can handle it as long as we're together. Anything. Which is why I'm here today asking you if you will please do me the very big honor of being my wife." Levi lifted the ring box a little higher. "Hope, will you marry me?"

"Yes!" She answered so quickly, it took Levi by surprise.

"Yes?"

"Yes." She nodded and laughed. Her hand shook, but Levi managed to slip the vintage diamond ring on her left hand. It was a perfect fit.

"It's beautiful, Levi." Hope stared at the ring while Levi got to his feet. "Is it your grandmother's?"

He nodded, suddenly overcome with emotion.

"It's absolutely perfect."

It was. But not as perfect as her.

Levi cupped her cheek for a moment before taking her into his arms and doing the one thing he'd been wanting to do since he'd set eyes on her. He pressed his lips to hers and kissed the love of his life.

Chapter Fourteen

"HEY, HEY."

A voice from behind her interrupted the moment. Not that either of them cared. Levi didn't release her from his embrace, a fact Hope was very grateful for.

"Seriously, I'm sorry to interrupt, but…" The voice that she now clearly recognized as Logan's interrupted them again. "Don't you guys need to say some vows or something first?"

Vows?

The dress.

The ring.

The people.

Realization dawned on her all at once as finally, belatedly, all of the pieces came together. Not only was Levi asking her to marry him, they *were* getting married. *Now.*

Hope pulled away and for the first time, looked at the people who up until that moment had been sitting quietly. Now, as she looked around at all her friends and neighbors, a buzz started to rise from the crowd.

"Wait." Hope looked to Levi, who beamed proudly. "What is happening here?"

"Well, you look the part, and everyone is here in your favorite ceremony location, and I just thought…"

"You thought what?"

"Well, you did say you'd marry me." He winked and she laughed.

"I guess I did."

"So why wait then? I'm here, you're here, all our friends are here, and we both look damn good." Levi waved an arm around the space, encompassing everything.

"It really is perfect." Hope had to agree. She'd planned and executed so many weddings over the years, and she'd be lying if she said that in all that time she hadn't imagined her own special day once or twice. Or ten or twenty times. "But, wait…" Hope shook her head as a complication popped into her head. "What about the license? We need a marriage license."

Levi grinned and gestured with his head. She turned to find Faith nearby with a smug smile on her face. "Don't tell me," Hope started. "Did you pull the twin thing?"

Faith shrugged. "You told me not to tell you." She laughed. "But I will say, there are still perks to being an identical twin. I just borrowed your ID is all. It's no biggie."

Hope laughed. "It very much is a biggie." She swallowed her laughter as tears threatened to replace the mirth. "You did all this?" she asked her sister.

Faith shook her head and pointed to Levi. "All I did was help. This was all him."

She couldn't be sure whether she was imagining it or not, but it certainly looked like there were tears shining in her sister's eyes. Her sister who didn't believe in love. She released Levi's hand long enough to pull her sister into a hug. "Thank you," Hope whispered in her ear. "Thank you so much for doing this."

"I told you—"

"I know what you said." Hope leaned back and looked into the eyes that were identical to her own. "But I also know what you did. So, thank you."

"I love you, Hope, and I just want what's best for you. You know that."

"I do."

"Can we get this show on the road?" Logan called out, and Faith groaned and rolled her eyes.

"He really is an asshole, isn't he?"

Hope laughed. "He's not a bad guy. Give him a chance."

"I'd really rather not." Faith's mouth pressed into a thin line while she looked in his direction, but then she shook her head and a smile replaced the frown. "Are you good with this?"

Hope turned and looked back at Levi, who watched them closely. She winked at him before answering her sister. "Totally."

It was a short ceremony, but absolutely perfect as they declared their love for each other in front of their witnesses. Hope had never been so completely happy as she was in the moment when she said *I do* and kissed her groom for the first time.

A cheer rose from the crowd before they turned to dance their way down the aisle. "That was absolutely perfect," she said to her new husband the moment they were out of earshot.

"I hope you don't really think that's it?"

Hope gave him a look. "What do you mean?"

"Come on, Hope. You're a wedding planner. Surely you should know that there's more to a wedding than the vows." He winked at her and took her hand as he led her to the golf cart. "We have a reception to get to."

"You didn't?"

She stared at him and shook her head in wonder as he moved to the driver's seat. *How had he pulled off an entire wedding and she hadn't even noticed?* It was impossible. She noticed every-thing that went on at the ranch.

Except in the last week or so.

Even she had to admit that she'd been distracted by her life lately.

"Of course I did."

But instead of taking her directly to the barn for the recep-tion he'd promised her, Levi whisked her through the woods in the opposite direction. Hope didn't ask where they were going, because she didn't care. As long as she was with Levi, she was perfectly happy.

And she was.

For the first time since that first trip to the doctor. Probably even longer. Hope glanced over at Levi sitting next to her. Her husband.

Husband.

Even thinking the word made her smile.

Yes, it had been a very long time since she'd been so happy.

Levi drove them across the property to a quiet, treed spot with a perfect grassy clearing on the riverbank.

"Remember this place?" Levi took her hand and helped her out of the golf cart.

"Of course."

It was *their* place. When they were teenagers, madly in love and desperate to be alone in a small town that didn't leave many places to sneak away, they'd gone to the river. Hope hadn't told anyone about their secret spot. Not even Faith. Whenever they could, Levi and Hope would sneak away to lay under the stars, talk about the future—their hopes and dreams —and clumsily, but enthusiastically, make love.

It was a special place and one Hope had avoided for many years.

Levi led her to the clearing and turned to take both her hands in his. "How do you feel?"

"About...all of this?"

He nodded.

"So good." It was the truth. "So happy, Levi. Really."

"Good." He kissed her gently. "I always want you to feel good. I vow to you to spend the rest of our lives, making you happy."

She smiled, but at the same time, she couldn't ignore the little twinge of sadness deep inside. It had been such a whirlwind day that they hadn't really had a chance to discuss a lot of the things that they needed to. Hope dropped her gaze to her feet. *Was she being naive? Had she been so swept up in the romance of the moment that she'd completely lost sight of the situation?*

"Levi, I..." She looked up into the eyes of the man she loved. "We should talk."

"About the honeymoon?" He was trying for humor and as much as Hope didn't want to ruin the moment by bringing reality into it, she had to.

"About everything."

"We do," Levi said, his voice dropping the humor. "I've been doing a lot of thinking, and I have another proposal for you."

She couldn't help but laugh this time. "Two in one day? I don't know if I can handle it."

"You can." He winked. "I'm sure of it."

"Okay, hit me." She squeezed her eyes shut and grinned. "What's your proposal?"

"Let's make a baby and travel the world."

Whatever she'd been expecting him to say, that wasn't it. Her eyes opened wide at the same moment her mouth fell open. "What? You want to...what?"

Levi cupped her cheek and looked straight into her eyes. "You want a baby," he said. "I want a baby. And if the doctors agree that it's safe, then let's do it."

"But you want—"

"You." He cut her off. "Remember? I want *you*. And I want everything with you. A baby, travel, settling down—a *life*, Hope. That's what I want. I need you to be able to understand that, okay? No more deciding what I want for me, okay?"

She nodded. "So you think…"

"I think we should have it all." He smiled. "Let's get on a plane and see the world, while we make a baby. There'll be plenty of time to come home and settle in before the baby comes." His eyes flashed with excitement. "There's never going to be a perfect time to do it," he continued. "But after the baby comes, there'll be new complications plus your treatment." Levi's eyes grew serious. "Your health comes first, Hope. Over everything. But I think we can make this work."

He sounded so sure of himself, so sure of his plan. *Could they really have it all? A baby and travel and a healthy life together?*

Levi certainly thought so, and so did she.

"I think it sounds amazing. Let's do it."

"Really?"

"You sound surprised."

"I am." He pulled her into his arms. "I was ready with all kinds of arguments about why it was a good idea."

"Well, you don't need them." She nuzzled in closer to him. "Because I totally agree with you. It sounds perfect."

"You pulled it off, cousin." Logan handed Levi a bottle of beer and leaned up against the bar next to him.

The wedding reception was in full swing and Logan was right—he had definitely pulled it off, but not alone. He'd had help. A lot of it.

"Thanks for all your help, Logan." He clinked his bottle together with his cousin's. "I don't think I could have done it without you."

Logan chuckled. "This was all you, buddy. And Faith. I was just manual labor."

Levi's eyes followed Logan's to the dance floor, where his new bride was dancing with her sister. He snuck a look back at his cousin, who watched Faith with a very strange look. One he'd seen on him before, many years ago. "Don't tell me you still have a thing for her."

Logan almost spat out the beer he'd been drinking. "What?" He managed to get the word out. "What are you talking about? Faith? No. I've never had a thing for her."

Levi raised his eyebrows and shrugged.

"No," Logan said again. "That's totally not a thing. Besides, she's just temporary, and I have no interest in getting involved in anyone whose plans involve living in the city."

"Interesting." Levi lifted the bottle to his mouth. "Because you have never mentioned getting involved with anyone. Ever. At least not until now."

"That's not what I meant." Logan's face went red. "I just meant—besides, she's seeing someone in the city."

There was definitely more to what Logan was saying than he was letting on, but Levi decided not to push his luck with his cousin. It probably wouldn't go over well if he ended up sporting a black eye on his wedding day.

"As long as you two can work together," Levi said. "I don't care what else goes on between the two of you."

He said it casually, but despite his attempt to slide it past his cousin, Logan wasn't letting anything slide. He stood up straight and stared at Levi. "What exactly are you talking about? *Work* together?"

"Who's working together?"

In exquisite timing, Faith and Hope had chosen that moment to leave the dance floor and join them. Levi wrapped an arm around his new wife—*wife;* he'd never get tired of that

—and pulled her close to his side. "I was just about to tell Logan about our plans."

"Plans?" Faith glanced between all of them. Her gaze landed back on Levi. "What kind of plans? Like a honeymoon?"

"Sort of." Hope shrugged. "We were actually going to wait to talk to you about this another time, but I guess there's no time quite like the present."

"Will someone just tell me what's going on?"

Levi took a breath, smiled at Hope, and told them what they were thinking. "Hope and I have decided to do some traveling while we start a family and then, before the baby is born, we'll come back and settle in."

Faith stared at both of them, and looked to Logan, who shrugged. Finally she spoke. "What about your…your treatment, Hope?" She leaned in and whispered the last part, not wanting to be overheard. A lot of people still didn't know about Hope's diagnosis, although that would have to change. "You can't just leave, Hope. What about the doctors and—"

"Don't worry." Hope held one hand out to her sister. "I promise you I'll do everything under doctor supervision." She glanced up at Levi, and his heart squeezed with love for the woman and how readily she'd accepted his plan. "But the doctor has already given me the all clear to go ahead and have a child before I have the surgery, so Levi suggested that while we try for that baby, and maybe for the first few months of the pregnancy, we do some traveling. It's all perfectly safe. And then we can have the best of both worlds and still be able to come home and settle in for the baby. And then I'll have the surgery," she added, mostly for Faith's benefit.

Faith shook her head back and forth as she took it all in. "Okay," she said slowly. "You know how I feel about it all, but you also know I'll support whatever you want. I just want you to be happy, Hope."

Levi watched as the sisters hugged, and Hope brushed a few tears from her eyes as she pulled back. "I'm really glad you said that, Faith. Because there's more."

"More?" Faith sighed and shook her head. "I have a feeling I'm not going to like this."

Hope grinned, but Levi was pretty sure Faith was right; she probably wasn't going to like what was coming next, but he hoped that she'd be okay with it anyway. The plan would still work if she wasn't, but it would be so much easier if she was, and it would make Hope happy.

"I was hoping..." Hope hesitated and looked back at Levi, who nodded and took her hand. "*We* were hoping," she started again. "That since you've been such a huge help here already and you seem to have adapted to it all really well, and—"

"You want me to stay and help you with the business?"

"Yes," Hope answered quickly. "I mean, no. Not really. I want you to run it." She dropped the bombshell. "Completely."

Levi watched as Faith absorbed what her sister had just said to her. "Run it?" she asked. "Completely?"

Hope nodded. "Completely," she confirmed. "But not just that, I want you to be a partner. *My* partner."

"Partner?" Faith looked around at the small group that was gathered. Around them, the wedding festivities continued as their friends and family danced and celebrated. It was the wedding that Faith put together in short notice. If there was ever any proof that she was capable of doing the job, they were standing in the middle of it. "I don't...I don't..."

"Don't answer now," Hope jumped in. "We shouldn't have even mentioned it today." She glanced back at Levi and smiled. She wasn't worried, and neither was he. This just felt right and he was confident that Faith would see it, too.

"Whoa." Logan, who'd remained largely quiet up until that

point, stepped forward. "You said a minute ago that we'd need to work together."

Dammit. Levi had been hoping he wouldn't bring that up.

"What did you mean by that?" Logan looked directly at him. "Why would we need to work together?"

"What?" Faith choked out the word and Levi vaguely noticed Logan offering her his beer, but she pushed his hand away. "What are you talking about? If you think for a minute that I'm going to—"

"I think I hear our song!" Hope grabbed Levi's hand and tugged. "Excuse me while I take my new husband for a dance."

Levi couldn't help but laugh once they were a safe distance away, and he spun his wife into his arms on the dance floor. He'd dodged a bullet, and they all knew it. They also all knew that there was going to be a difficult conversation at some point. But that point wasn't now, so he turned his back on his cousin and his new sister-in-law, and put all his focus on the only thing that really mattered at that very moment.

His wife.

Chapter Fifteen

FAITH WENT over the calendar in front of her again. She'd already gone over it four times but despite the repetition, it wasn't looking any easier. In fact, it might just be looking harder and more impossible than it had when she'd agreed to take over the operations of Ever After Ranch.

A decision she was rapidly beginning to regret.

"I don't know about this." She shook her head and spoke aloud to no one in particular. "There's no way I can do this."

"Of course there is."

Faith looked up to see Hope, a smile on her face as she walked into the kitchen. Faith was pretty sure her sister hadn't stopped smiling since the surprise wedding three days earlier. It was nice to see. Really nice. But her sister's happiness didn't make it any easier to accept the fact that she may have just made the worst decision of her life in accepting Hope's partnership offer.

Faith shook her head. "I don't really see how. This schedule is crazy. How do you do this?" She looked back to the schedule and started making mental lists of all the things she'd need to take care of in order to pull off an entire season's worth of weddings on her own. "Do you really think it's fair to the brides?" she asked without looking up. "I mean, they booked their wedding when they thought that you were going to be executing their special day. I'm hardly a worthy substitute."

Hope put her hands on Faith's shoulders and squeezed. "I don't want to ask you if you're sure about your decision," she said. "Because I don't want you to change your mind." Her sister's voice was laced with concern and the slightest bit of worry, and immediately Faith felt bad. The last thing she wanted was for Hope to worry about her business or her while she was gone on her trip. It was important that she and Levi go on this trip and enjoy every single moment of it without any concern for what was going on at home. The only thing they needed to worry about was making a baby.

As much as Faith didn't like the idea of her sister putting her treatment off to have a child, it was important to Hope, and whatever was important to Hope was important to her. Besides, Faith trusted Levi, and she knew he'd make sure she was safe and healthy.

"I won't change my mind," Faith said with certainty. "I made you a promise, and I'll keep it. But it doesn't mean I'm not scared shitless."

Hope laughed and sat next to her at the table. "You know I'm only a phone call away. Besides, Logan agreed to help out as much as he possibly can."

That was a whole different problem. Faith shook her head. Logan was nothing but trouble, as far as she was concerned. He always had been. He was a partier and a troublemaker. They'd always rubbed each other the wrong way, and Faith couldn't see why it would be any different to work with him now than it was when they were younger.

Nothing had changed.

Especially the slightest bit of sexual tension between them.

She shook her head in an effort to clear it. That was the real problem. Despite the fact that she found Logan Langdon incredibly annoying and a giant pain in her ass, she couldn't help the intense feelings of desire that he sparked in her. And those feelings definitely hadn't lessened over the years.

"I don't know if working with Logan is a good idea," Faith admitted. "I think I might be better off on my own, to be honest. I don't really need—"

"Do you remember when you were telling me how badly I needed help?"

She nodded. Of course she remembered.

"If I needed help, you absolutely will, Faith. And that's okay. It's a big job. Too much for one person, but I know you're up to the challenge."

Faith laughed. "I'm glad you have confidence in me."

"Are you kidding me? Of course I do. Not only are you a kick-ass paralegal, you're my sister and you can do anything. Even weddings."

"Even weddings," she repeated. "I mean, I better be good at weddings, because I guess I'm not a paralegal anymore."

The day before, Faith had called and put in her official notice at the firm. Like a coward, she'd called human resources to tell them the news first. Judging by the amount of voicemails and texts on her phone in the last twenty-four hours, the secret was out and Noah had heard the news, too. She'd tried to tell herself that she'd done the right thing, that they were never supposed to be anything serious, and that she didn't owe him anything. But despite every single thing she told herself, she couldn't bring herself to actually believe it.

"About that," Hope said. "How do you feel about it all?"

"About leaving the firm?"

"No," Hope said with a small smile. "About leaving the guy."

The guy.

They'd never actually talked about Noah, but that didn't mean that her sister didn't know something was up. Say what you want about twin intuition, but it was a very real thing. Hope knew her better than anyone. Maybe even herself some days.

Faith dropped her gaze to the table and answered honestly. "I don't know." She shook her head. "I miss him, but at the same time, it wasn't anything serious."

"So you keep saying." Hope reached over and put her hand over Faith's. "It's okay to have feelings about this, you know."

She looked at her sister. *Was that really true? Was it okay to have feelings about it when she was the one who'd insisted on keeping feelings out of it in the first place?* And was she really even having feelings about it at all, or was she just stressed and overwhelmed about the changes that were going on? After all, packing up and moving back to her hometown to run a business she didn't fully believe in because your twin sister, and only living family member, had cancer and instead of seeking immediate treatment was going traveling around the world while trying to have a baby was a lot to take in. That *was* a lot. Which was probably what was really going on. It wasn't that she missed Noah, or had *feelings* for him or the fact that she was officially breaking off whatever it was that they had when they weren't supposed to have anything at all.

She was overwhelmed. That was all.

Faith shook her head and forced a smile. "I'm fine. And this whole situation is fine."

Hope laughed. "Is it?"

"No!" Faith laughed too. "It's not fine at all. But it will be. Because the most important thing is that *you* will be fine. Now, don't you have some packing to do or something?"

. . .

"She doesn't want me here." Logan grunted as he stacked the chairs while Levi looked on.

He'd been watching his cousin work for the last twenty minutes, and in that time Logan hadn't stopped talking about Faith. It would be funny if Levi wasn't actually concerned about the state of his new wife's business while they went on their trip. Deep down, he was sure it would be fine. Well, mostly sure, but he still had his doubts about Faith running things, especially with Logan as her *general labor*. The two of them could barely exist in the same room without throwing barbs at each other; what were the odds that they'd be able to get through an entire wedding without breaking into a fight that guaranteed the bride and groom remembered their special day for entirely the wrong reasons?

Levi certainly wasn't putting money on it.

"She'll get used to it."

"No," Logan insisted. "She won't." He stacked another chair and turned to look at Levi as he wiped his hands together. "Earlier, she saw me in here and I thought she was actually going to throw one of those glass things at me."

Levi glanced in the direction Logan was pointing to. "A vase?" he asked with an eye roll. "You thought she was going to throw a vase at you?"

"Yes."

Levi had to work hard not to laugh out loud. His cousin definitely had a flair for the dramatic. Especially where Faith was concerned.

"And what did you do or say to deserve that?"

He also knew his cousin well, and knew that there was no way Logan *hadn't* said or done something.

"Nothing."

Levi narrowed his eyes and tipped his head.

"Well, I might have said something about her ass."

"Her *ass?*" Levi's mouth fell open. Even for Logan, that was a bit too far. He'd always liked to push Faith's buttons, but there was a line. "Logan. You can't talk about her ass. Too far."

Logan shrugged. "Well, 1 complimented it at least."

Again, Levi looked at him skeptically.

"Okay," Logan confessed. "I said that her ass didn't look quite as hard in the jeans she was wearing. I mean, for a hard ass, that's a compliment, right?"

Levi groaned and dipped his head in an effort to cover his laughter from his cousin. Finally, he was able to pull himself together. "Logan, come on. Can you at least try? For me? For Hope?"

Logan didn't answer, but shrugged and walked across the room to start stacking a new set of chairs. "I said I'd help out," he said. "But it doesn't mean it's going to be easy."

Levi couldn't help but think there was more to it than what Logan was saying. But there was nothing to be gained from prying into his cousin's affairs the night before he was set to get on a plane and start the honeymoon of a lifetime with his new wife.

It still gave him a little thrill to think of Hope as his wife. Finally. He should have married her years ago. Not that he had any regrets. None at all. Everything worked out the way it was supposed to. Just like things would work out with Logan and Faith at the ranch while they were gone.

He glanced over at his cousin again and shook his head. Well, at least he could hope that everything would work out.

"Do you have any more questions for me about what to do around here?"

Logan shook his head. "Not unless you can tell me how to get Faith on my good side."

Levi laughed. "Maybe you could start by not calling her a hard ass, or referring to her ass at all."

Logan looked at him as if he were considering it before

shaking his head and laughing. "Nah. That won't work."

His cousin was nothing if not consistent. "Well, at the very least, try not to piss her off tonight, okay? Wait until I get Hope on a plane and out of here before you go to war with her sister. I want Hope to feel okay about leaving Ever After Ranch in *capable* hands." He used air quotes and shook his head when Logan shrugged.

"I'll do my best. Now get out of here so I can finish this up and get to your farewell dinner."

Levi couldn't argue with that. Besides, it did look like his cousin had a solid grasp on what was going on with the upcoming weddings. No doubt there'd be a few bumps along the road, but Levi was confident that Faith would be able to handle it. She'd be able to handle Logan, too. He was certain of it, even if it was the last thing she might want to do. Faith would get him in line.

On his way back up to the house, he spotted his new sister-in-law walking alone in the direction of the river. He waved at her, but she either didn't see him or was ignoring him. Either way, he'd see her soon enough. They'd planned one last family dinner at the house before he and Hope got on the plane in the morning and began the first leg of their journey.

That was, if Hope ever finished packing.

"Hey there, Mrs. Langdon." He wrapped his arms around his beautiful wife as she stood in front of her closet and hugged her tight. "I am never going to get tired of saying that." He kissed her neck and she moaned a little as she leaned into his attentions.

"And I'm never going to get tired of hearing it." Hope turned in his arms and kissed him deeply. "I'm glad I decided to take your name."

"Me too." He gave her another kiss. "But you know I would have been fine if you hadn't."

"I know." She smiled at him and he couldn't help but kiss

her again. "What are you up to? Are Aunt Debbie and Katie here yet?" She wiggled out of his arms before he could kiss her yet again and grabbed a handful of T-shirts. "Katie said she was going to sweet-talk Brody into packing us up a lasagna and some salads on her way over so we didn't have to cook anything."

"That would be delicious." Levi's stomach growled. Delicious would be an understatement. Brody Morris took over as the head chef at Birchwood while Levi had been out of town. Although it had been a good restaurant before, now it was absolutely amazing. Pretty much everything Brody cooked was five stars. Lasagna would be a treat considering they were about to spend the next few days eating nothing but airline food.

"Are you still packing?" Levi flopped down on the bed and assessed what his wife had collected. "There is way too much here." He shook his head. "I told you a million times, Hope. You don't need much. Just pack what can fit in the backpack. You don't want to be lugging a suitcase all over the place."

"I know, I know."

He looked at her in question, because it certainly didn't look like she *knew*. He picked up a pair of black high heels in front of him. "You definitely won't need these. I can't imagine there will be many cocktail parties to attend in Thailand."

"You never know." She snatched the shoes away from him and laughed.

"Oh, I know."

Everything had moved so quickly in the days after the wedding. They'd settled on a rough itinerary, trading in their Mexico tickets so they could start in Asia, before moving over to New Zealand and Australia. If time permitted, depending on Hope's health and how the baby-making went, they'd head over to Europe for a few months before coming back to the ranch and settling in. It was an ambitious schedule to be sure, but Levi had wanted to fit in as much as possible before starting a family. With such a tight timeline, they were going to be on the move a lot. Packing light would definitely help.

"I promise I'll scale things back," Hope said, as if she'd read his mind. "I'm just starting with everything and slowly weeding things out."

"Okay."

"You don't look like you believe me."

Levi hoisted himself off the bed. "I'll believe it when I see it, babe. But either way, make sure you're ready to go in the morning. Because ready or not, we're doing this."

Once again, he pulled his wife into his arms and kissed her thoroughly. "You are ready for this, aren't you? I know everything has happened really quickly. I just want to make sure that—"

"I'm good." She cut him off. "I really am. And now that Doctor Barrett has given us the all clear, not even Faith can protest this." She shrugged. "Well, she can't protest too much, anyway. But honestly, I'm good. This is amazing. It's all amazing. I know Faith is feeling a little overwhelmed right now, but she's going to be so great at this." Hope's mouth pressed into a line. "And I think it will be good for her, too."

"What do you mean by that?"

"There's something going on with her," Hope said. "I don't really know how to explain it, but even having her home for the last few weeks, she's changed. I think that being at the ranch and running things on her own for a bit will help her with some clarity."

"Babe, there's been something going on with Faith for a long time." Levi didn't mean for it to sound insensitive, not at all. But it was true. It was clear to anyone who knew her well that Faith had been running away from something for a long time. "I hope this really is as good for her as we think it will be."

Hope nodded. "And I hope she deals with whatever, or I should say, whomever it is in the city that she needs to deal with." Hope shook her head. "She won't talk about it, but she did tell me she had a call to make."

"Maybe that's where she was going," Levi suggested. "As I came in, I saw her heading toward the river. I thought she was going for a walk, but—"

"No. She was going to our spot." A small, knowing smile crossed Hope's face. "I thought maybe she'd forgotten about it. Getting out there will help her figure things out."

Levi looked at her in confusion. "How do you know that? How could a spot by the river possibly help anything?"

Hope laughed and kissed him quickly on the nose. "Because it's home."

Faith hadn't been to the special spot by the river since she was a teenager. It had been hers and Hope's spot. At some point over the years, when everything changed for her, she'd stopped going. It was as if she'd stopped believing in magic altogether the day she discovered that love wasn't a real thing but just a line that people told to get what they wanted.

Even thinking about it made her feel jaded and bitter. And maybe it wasn't really all that bad. After all, Hope and Levi were in love and that story had definitely had a happy ever after.

Did it?

She hated herself for being skeptical, but she couldn't help it. Sure, Hope and Levi were happy now, but it had been a long road to get there, and who knew how long it would last.

"No." She spoke aloud even though she was completely alone. She may be a non-believer, but it was like Santa: just because she didn't believe, didn't mean that others couldn't.

And she refused to let any negative feelings creep in where Hope was concerned.

Besides, that's not why she'd come out to the river to be alone.

Faith let out a deep breath as she pushed through the branches on the trail that led to her special place. It was exactly the same as she'd remembered it during all of those yoga classes when the instructor told her to close her eyes and picture a calm, safe space.

A smile crossed her face as she made her way to the riverbank and sat.

She closed her eyes and breathed in deeply, inhaling the familiar scent of grass and the distinct scent of fresh water.

The sense of calm washed over her just like the water flowing over the rocks.

Finally, she was home.

Home.

Was the ranch really home? Could it be? Her condo in the city had never really felt like home. It had always just had the slightest sense of temporary. But Ever After Ranch had to be temporary too. There was no way she could settle here. Not permanently.

Hell, it was pushing every single one of her boundaries to commit to staying for the next—however many—months. Because no one really knew how long Hope and Levi would be gone. But even with such an open-ended offer, there was no way she could have said no.

It didn't matter what she had back in the city. A job? Not important. A condo? She'd get rid of it. A man? He'd understand.

None of it was even remotely as important as what Hope was going through. And she was her twin sister. Her only living family member. Faith would do anything for her. It didn't matter. None of the other stuff mattered.

The man.

Noah.

Shit.

Maybe that was the one thing that mattered. Just a little.

She'd done her best over the last few weeks to let him down gently, but he wasn't taking the hint. He still called and texted every day. It was almost like he had feelings for her. Which was not the deal. Not. Even. Close.

Faith pulled her cell phone from her pocket and squeezed her eyes shut as she inhaled deeply.

It would be so easy to just keep ignoring his texts and messages. But that wasn't okay and she knew it. Besides, overnight she'd taken over the operations of a wedding planning business. Hell, if anyone could do hard things, *she* could do hard things.

Before she could chicken out, Faith dialed his number, and like a chicken shit prayed silently that it would go to voicemail.

"Hello? Faith?"

Shit.

"Hey, Noah. I'm glad I caught you."

"Are you?"

Yes. No. She took a deep breath but before she could answer, Noah continued. "I miss you, Faith. I know you said it wasn't supposed to be anything—"

"Noah, please."

"Please what?"

Please don't tell me you love me. Please don't tell me you miss me. Please don't tell me anything that will make this harder because I... "Please listen to me." It was such a cop-out, and there was no doubt they both knew it. "I have to tell you something."

"Are you going to tell me what the hell is going on?" There was an edge to his voice that she'd never heard before. "Because one day you say you're going to go help your sister for a few days and then you tell me it's over and then you stop answering my calls and then I have to find out from management that you quit your job! So seriously, Faith. What the hell is going on?"

Faith exhaled slowly. "I'm moving here, Noah. There's been a lot going on and I can't get into it right now, but I need to stay here and run the ranch for the foreseeable future. You and I were never going to...well, I told you how I felt about relationships, so it's not like I'm breaking any promises or anything." The words came out in a jumble, but she couldn't stop herself. "Even so, I thought you deserved to hear it from me."

"What? You're going to *stay*?"

There was so much hurt and confusion in his voice that something inside Faith's heart clenched.

"I'm sorry, Noah." And she was. More than even she thought she would be. *So* sorry. A hot and totally unexpected tear pricked at the corner of her eye. *Oh hell no!* She would not cry. No way. "It all happened so fast and—"

"I love you, Faith."

No. No. No. She shook her head as the tear slipped down her cheek.

"You don't."

"I do." She thought she heard his voice crack on the other end of the line. But then he cleared his throat and when he spoke again, the hard edge had returned. "I do love you, Faith. More than you might ever know. And that's such a shame, because as much as you say you don't believe in it, you do, Faith. You *do* believe in love. You're just too damn stubborn and hardheaded to see it when it's right in front of your eyes."

"Noah, I—"

"You know what?" He cut her off again. "Maybe you're right." He chuckled, but there was no humor in it. "Maybe this can't happen. Good-bye, Faith."

She held the phone to her ear long after he'd disconnected

the call and then, when she was sure he wasn't there anymore, Faith dropped her phone to the ground, hugged her legs and let herself cry. She cried for more than the loss of a relationship she'd never planned on having, but also for her sister, the stress of uprooting her life, and months—maybe years—of holding in her feelings.

When finally there were no more tears, she stood and stretched her arms over her head. She felt drained, but also rejuvenated. Maybe the ranch would be the fresh start she didn't even know she needed.

And there was only one way to find out.

She straightened her clothes and with one last look over the river, headed back through the trees and to the house, where everyone would be waiting to have the big going-away dinner.

Tomorrow, Hope and Levi would be gone and then it was sink or swim. She might as well soak in as much information as she possibly could.

Thirty minutes later, everyone was gathered around the old oak table in the kitchen. They were passing around a huge dish of the most delicious lasagna Faith had ever tasted. "Where did you say this was from?" she asked with a mouth full.

"Birchwood," Aunt Deb answered as she passed the dish back in Faith's direction. "Brody Morris is the head chef over there and he's absolutely the best thing to happen to that restaurant in decades. But don't you tell Burt and Josie Michaels," she added. "They ran that place since it opened and while I'm not going to complain about the many meals we enjoyed there over the years, they had nothing on Brody Morris."

"Did you ever meet Brody, Faith?" Hope asked from the other side of the table. "I think he moved to town while you were away. He's done some catering for us over the years, too.

But now he's so busy with the restaurant. You should go say hi, though. He's a good ally to have."

"And he's hot." Katie fanned herself with her napkin and Faith laughed.

"Hot?"

"So hot."

"I hardly think he's *hot.*" Logan stuffed a piece of garlic bread in his mouth.

"I'd have some questions for you if you did, brother." Katie elbowed him in the side and Logan coughed hard as he choked down his bread.

"I'm just saying that I hardly think Faith will find…never mind. It doesn't matter." He picked up his beer and drank deeply.

But Faith couldn't help but notice the slightest red flush that had appeared on his cheeks.

She shook her head and turned away. No doubt he was just looking for another thing to bug her about. It was going to be a long—well, for however long—working with him if she didn't learn how to ignore him. She couldn't keep letting him get to her.

"I'll make it a point to introduce myself," Faith said to Hope.

"Apparently Brody's coaching Sarah's little girl's soccer team," Hope said. "Maybe you can—"

"Check out the town's soccer team?" Faith laughed. "Or at the very least, the coach." She threw in the last comment only to see whether Logan would react. His jaw tightened, and she felt the slightest sense of satisfaction, although she couldn't have explained why.

"Soccer's a stupid sport," Logan muttered under his breath.

Yes, she'd definitely gotten a reaction.

"Tell us again about your trip," Aunt Debbie said in a very

smooth effort to distract the attention from her son. "I need to live vicariously through you both."

"Don't worry, Aunt Debbie," Levi said. "We'll make sure to FaceTime you and show you all the—"

"FaceTime." Debbie wrinkled up her nose. "How about an old-fashioned postcard? Doesn't anyone send those anymore?"

Hope and Levi looked at each other in question, and Faith couldn't help but laugh.

"I'm sure they do, Debbie," Hope said after a moment. "I promise I'll find them wherever I can and send them back to you."

"Good." Debbie looked satisfied and they dissolved into conversation about Hope and Levi's itinerary. It was jam-packed and even though she knew her sister wouldn't say anything, Faith knew that Hope was a little nervous about it. She'd never really traveled before and now, instead of easing into it, Levi was grabbing her hand and diving straight into the deep end. Of course she was nervous.

But Faith knew she'd be fine. Hell, her sister would be more than fine. She'd thrive with the adventure and no doubt she'd come home a changed person. The idea made Faith a little sad, but it was probably just her ridiculously heightened emotions from everything that had happened in the last few days, and she pushed the feeling away. This trip would be nothing but great for everyone.

Except maybe her.

She shook her head and looked down at her plate.

"What's up, Faith?"

Her head snapped up. "Nothing," she said quickly.

"Sure doesn't look like nothing."

She spun in her chair and glared at Logan. "I'll show *you*—"

"Okay, okay," Levi jumped in. "You're not allowed to kill each other while we're still here."

"Right?" Hope laughed. "At least wait until we're on the plane."

Everyone laughed except Faith and Logan, who looked at each other and shook their heads.

At least they agreed on one thing. Their family was too much. Way too much.

"Whatever," Faith said, changing the subject. "I've been looking over the appointment book for the next few months and I'm happy to see that you didn't book it totally solid." It was a small miracle that her sister hadn't booked weddings into every spare second, but she'd take it.

"I thought you'd like that." Hope grinned before taking another bite of her dinner. "It shouldn't be too much for you. Besides," she added, "I'm more than confident after I saw what you could pull off in only a few days that you will knock this season out of the park."

Faith couldn't help but feel a little glow of satisfaction deep inside. Sure, weddings were the last thing she wanted to be doing, but if she was stuck at Ever After Ranch doing them, there was very little doubt that she'd do the very best she could.

"Hey," Katie said from the other side of the table. "Speaking of weddings."

They all stared at her. "I don't know if you've noticed," Logan said, "but that's *all* we talk about around here?"

Katie laughed and waved her hand. "Yeah, yeah, but specifically…" She looked at Faith. "You said that you weren't totally booked up this season?"

Faith shrugged and nodded. "It looks that way. Why?"

"Do you have a date next month?"

Faith narrowed her eyes at her friend. "I'm sure I do," she said cautiously. "Why?"

"Do you remember my friend Damon Banks?"

"Of course," Debbie said. "You two were inseparable all through school." She smiled in memory. "I remember the day you two met. I picked you up from school. You were in first grade, I believe…" Katie nodded. "And you could not stop talking about the little boy who'd just moved to town and how much you hated him."

"I did!"

Debbie gave her a look.

"I did, Mom. He pulled my braids and threw erasers at me. It went on for weeks." Debbie laughed, but Katie ignored her. "But when he tried to take my cookie at recess…" Katie pressed her lips together and shook her head. "That was crossing a line."

"And if I remember correctly, that was the day the principal called because you'd punched poor little Damon Banks in the nose and made it bleed."

Faith started laughing as the story was recalled. Katie was a sweet girl, and definitely led with love, but there was no doubt in her mind that she also wouldn't hesitate to stand up for herself and right a wrong. Or defend a cookie, as the case may be.

"Hey," Katie said in response to the laughter. "It was a really good cookie."

"I was so proud." Logan raised his hand for a high five. "I taught her those moves."

Debbie shot her son a look, but it was clear that she wasn't upset with either of them. "After that, well, after the two-day suspension and the apology you had to give him, the two of you were inseparable. You did everything together."

They'd been two years behind her and Hope in school, but Faith remembered the pair of them well. It was true; they'd done everything together up until graduation when, last she'd heard, Damon had moved for college and had since invented some sort of computer chip that had made him millions.

"Whatever happened to him?" Debbie mused. "I suppose there's not much of a reason for him to come home to visit much. Not since his mother died. He was always so much closer to her, wasn't he? Damon and his dad never really saw eye to eye, that was for sure. But it's so sad that Anthony's out there on his property all alone. It's such a nice house. At least, it was."

It had been *the* house in high school. The oversized log cabin in the woods that was outfitted like a fancy house in the city, complete with a full-sized swimming pool, had been the scene of many parties while Damon's parents were out of town on one of their frequent trips. Faith had been to one or two, herself. It was an amazing house.

"Last I heard, Anthony wasn't well," Debbie continued. "He has some nurse or something coming in to care for him. He never was the same after Leona died. And to have a heart attack so young. So terrible."

They all fell into silence for a moment as they absorbed just how terrible that was, but a moment later, Debbie raised her head and looked at Katie. "Sorry, honey. I went off on a bit of a trip down memory lane there. What's going on with Damon these days?"

"He's getting married."

"Oh?" Debbie sat back in her chair. "That's exciting!"

"Wow. Good for him," Logan said. "Who's he marrying?"

Katie dabbed her napkin to her lips and dropped it on her plate before answering as matter-of-factly as she could. "Me."

———

I hope you enjoyed Ever After Ranch and Hope and Levi's second chance love story. There is a lot more love in store, including Katie's shocking wedding surprise, coming next in *Needing Happily Ever After*. Read on for a special sneak peek!

And if you want even more romance...click <u>HERE</u> for an exclusive FREE novella that isn't available anywhere else!

Needing Happily Ever After

Please enjoy this excerpt from the second in the Ever After Series—Needing Happily Ever After

There were probably a million ways that Katie Langdon could have told her family about her upcoming nuptials to Damon Banks. Particularly considering as far as anyone knew, she wasn't even dating Damon, and certainly the news was unexpected, to say the least.

She'd actually toyed with the idea of telling her mom privately first, but she couldn't help but feel that there was safety in numbers. Her mom may be slight, but she was tough and even her big brother Logan was smart enough not to piss Mom off.

Not that news of Katie's nuptials should *piss off* her mom, but it was sure to get a reaction. There didn't seem to be a very good way to share the news at all, so Katie made the split-second decision to just blurt it out in the middle of a family dinner. And not just any family dinner. No way. A going-away dinner for her cousin Levi and his new wife, Hope, who had been like a sister to her growing up. The two of them were scheduled to leave early the next morning on an extended honeymoon around the world—or a lot of it, anyway—so everyone was focused on them. No one would really pay much attention to her announcement.

At least, that had been her hope.

She'd been wrong. Very wrong.

Forks clattered to plates. Someone coughed. There was a sound somewhere between a choke and a laugh. She didn't want to look, but Katie was a little bit afraid that her mom had made a sobbing noise.

She sighed, and braced herself as the questions began.

"What are you talking about?"

"Married? Like, married married?"

"To Damon? Are you even dating?"

"Have you *ever* dated Damon?"

"He's your best friend."

The questions, really, were valid and all things that she herself would have asked if the roles were reversed. Still, she kept her answers as vague as possible.

"Marriage."

"Yes, married married."

"Yes, to Damon. We've been close our whole lives."

"Dating is such an old-fashioned idea."

"I love him very much."

It didn't matter that she'd never loved Damon *that* way. It was true, they'd been inseparable since grade one. Marriage would just make them even more inseparable. No one knew her better than Damon Banks.

Even so, her family did not look impressed.

Yes. She totally should have waited to tell them.

At least until Damon himself was in town.

Isn't that how people announced their engagements? With their betrothed by their side?

Hell, she didn't even have a ring.

Katie looked down at her lasagna, and took a deep breath before looking up with a smile on her face. She focused first at Faith Turner, who had a funny grin on her face. Hope's twin sister, Faith had also been like a big sister to Katie growing up, although she'd only recently moved back to Glacier Falls to take over her sister's wedding business at Ever After Ranch, which was the only reason Katie had brought up the whole *marriage thing* in the first place.

"You want to have your wedding at Ever After Ranch?" Faith put a bite of pasta in her mouth.

"No!" It was Logan, her big brother, who objected. "She is *not* getting married. Never mind at the ranch."

Faith rolled her eyes and kept looking at Katie, but Hope spoke next. "Do you want us to change our travel plans? If you're getting married right away, we'll—"

"No!" Levi interrupted. "I love you, Katie, you know that. But we are *not* changing our plans." He looked pointedly at his new wife. "We only have a limited time to do this before the baby and your treatment and...no." He shook his head and Hope nodded.

"No," Katie agreed. Hope had been recently diagnosed with uterine cancer, and her doctor had given her only a small window of time in order to attempt to conceive a child before she would need to have surgery to treat her disease. Their trip was too important. "You aren't changing your plans. But yes, I was hoping that maybe if there was an opening at the ranch..."

"No," Logan said again. "You aren't getting married."

"I am."

She still hadn't looked at her mother, but this time there was no mistaking the sound that escaped her mother's lips. She did not want to see her mom crying.

"It's really not a big deal." Katie knew the moment the words were out of her mouth, they were the wrong choice. She tried to quickly backpedal. "I mean, it *is* a big deal. Obviously. I mean, it's marriage. I know that. But I don't know why everyone is so surprised. It's Damon. And me and Damon are…well, we're me and Damon." She shrugged and took a bite of garlic bread as if to signal the end of the conversation.

Logan opened his mouth to say something else, but Faith stopped him with a hand on his arm. "Just leave it," she said. "Let's just get through dinner, okay?"

Her big brother looked as though he were going to explode, and Katie wouldn't have been surprised. Logan's relationship with Faith was contentious with a distinct undercurrent of sexual tension, but to her surprise, he nodded and turned his attention back to his dinner.

For a few moments, everyone focused on eating and the only sound to be heard was the scraping of cutlery against the plates. Finally, after what felt like an eternity, Hope started talking again about their upcoming trip and some of the activities they had planned. Soon enough, the tension had almost completely lifted and Katie could almost forget that she'd just dropped a bomb on her entire family.

Almost.

Because when she finally dared to look at her mother, Debbie Langdon was staring directly at Katie, a look of concern and question in her eyes. As much as Katie would like to believe that the hard part was over when it came to this whole thing, she wasn't foolish enough to believe her own bullshit. It was only just beginning.

At least she'd have Damon at her side to help field some of these questions. She shook her head and stuffed another bite of food in her mouth.

She really should have waited until he arrived to say anything at all. He'd been her best friend for almost twenty years and apparently nothing much had changed—he was still getting her into hot water.

Only this time, it seemed a little more serious than getting called to the principal's office.

Despite the stress and worry flooding through her, Katie worked hard to keep the smile on her face as she got through the rest of dinner. After all, she was a blushing bride-to-be.

Wasn't she?

#

Damon Banks couldn't remember exactly how long it had been since he'd been to his hometown of Glacier Falls.

Three years? Four?

No. It had been three.

They'd buried his mom four years ago. But he'd come back for a quick trip for Katie's twenty-first birthday the year after. And that had been three years ago already.

It was hard to believe it had been so long. Especially considering not much had changed in the small mountain town. Of course, nothing ever seemed to change in Glacier Falls. That's why he liked it so much.

He drove his newly purchased pickup truck down the highway that led to Main Street. There were one or two new houses and acreages set back in the trees, but so far, it all looked mostly the same.

Damon took the turn that led him off the main road right before heading into town onto Forester's Road. It wound its way up and away from the townsite below to a magnificent hilltop estate that looked over the windy river that wound its way through the valley and held a spectacular view of Jumbo Glacier tucked into the mountains in the distance. It also happened to be the site of his childhood home and the entire reason he was back in Glacier Falls.

Well, *half* the reason he was back.

There was Katie, too.

His *fiancée*.

It still felt strange to think that of his oldest and best friend that way, but he was going to have to get used to it. And quickly.

He pulled his truck off the road beside the main gates and killed the engine, but he didn't get out of the truck right away. Instead, he took a deep breath and ran his hands through his thick hair, almost as if to steel himself for what was outside. Which was ridiculous. There was nothing out there but pine trees, fresh air, and…beyond those gates somewhere, his father.

Damon was being childish and he knew it. He wasn't a teenager anymore, for God's sake. With a shake of his head, he opened the door and stretched his legs as he stepped onto the road. It was heavily treed, and from where he stood, there wasn't much of a view into the valley below. But he knew very well that just beyond the gates, down the lane, was an amazing view. His favorite view, really. It didn't matter where he went in the world, or what exotic locations his travels took him; nothing compared to the view from ElkView Ridge. Maybe it was a sense of home, or the good memories he held of the place, or even just the fact that it was familiar to him. But whenever he looked out over the mountaintops, something changed inside him. Almost as if a switch were flipped that allowed him to breathe again.

And that sense of breath and peace was just beyond the gates.

No doubt the code was the same as it always had been, too. But he didn't press the buttons on the keypad to enter the familiar numbers. Instead, he dropped his head and sighed.

Part of him wanted more than anything to walk into his childhood home the way he did for so many years, knock on his father's office door and say hello as casually as if he hadn't been gone for years and there wasn't a cavernous divide between them. And hadn't always been.

Damon couldn't actually remember a time when there hadn't been a strange distance between them. When his mother had been alive, the gap hadn't seemed quite so insurmountable. But after her death, it was as if the little bit of glue they did have holding them together died right along with her. Those days and weeks after her funeral had been so tense and uncomfortable in the house. If it weren't for his father expressing how disappointing Damon was to both of his parents, and how he'd *broken his mother's heart*, there wouldn't have been any conversation between them at all.

When he closed his eyes, he could still hear his father's voice in his ears.

"She died from a broken heart, Damon." His father's words had come out of nowhere over a dinner of leftover casserole some caring neighbor had brought over. "You left home and she didn't know what to do with herself."

"That's not my fault." Ever since the funeral, he'd tried his best to avoid a conversation like this one with his father, knowing exactly how it would go. "She had a heart attack, Dad. That's very different."

"She dedicated her whole life to loving you, and you just left," he continued, as if Damon hadn't spoken.

"I went to school, Dad. I'm in college."

Anthony Banks shook his head, not willing to hear any *excuses* from his son. "All she ever wanted was to see you settled down with a family, Damon."

"I'm barely twenty years old!" He finally raised his voice, and even as he did, Damon knew it was futile. "It's not my fault that she never got a chance to see that and you know it. I'm only sorry that she was stuck here alone with *you*." His father's face had gone sheet-white, and Damon knew he should stop himself, that saying hurtful things wouldn't bring his mother back. But he couldn't stop the next words as they flew from his mouth. "Did you ever think that maybe she died to get away from you?"

He regretted the hateful words the moment he spoke them,

but it was too late. They'd never been close, but Damon had never purposefully been hurtful. Shame flooded through him as his dad quietly got up from the table and left the room.

That was the last time they'd spoken properly. Not that there was anything proper about that conversation.

Besides a few terse conversations that Damon could count on one hand, he hadn't heard from his dad in years.

Until last week.

He'd memorized the email he'd received barely seven days ago.

Damon,

The time has come to sell ElkView Ridge. It will be formally listed in two weeks' time.

I thought you should know.

Dad

There was no way he was going to let his dad sell his home out from under him.

No. Way.

ElkView Ridge was the only place that had ever felt like home to him. The only place where he felt like *him*. And more importantly than that, it was his mother's home. *If it was gone…*

No. He wouldn't even let himself think about it.

Almost as soon as he'd received the email, Damon had called his lawyer to put in an offer on the property. Money wasn't an object. It hadn't been since he'd sold his microchip design in a bidding war with the top computing companies. No, whatever his dad wanted for ElkView Ridge, he'd pay it.

Only the lawyers didn't even get as far as putting in the offer because there was one major stipulation in the listing. One requirement that any potential buyer had to fulfill before an offer, no matter the size, would be considered.

Bastard.

And that was the real reason Damon had come back to town. To fulfill the criteria necessary to buy back his childhood home.

He turned his back on the heavy timber gate, and got back in his truck.

It was time to find Katie. And he was already late.

Needing Happily Ever After, Katie and Damon's story is next!

About the Author

Elena Aitken is a USA Today Bestselling Author of more than forty romance and women's fiction novels. The mother of 'grown up' twins, Elena now lives with her very own mountain man in the heart of the very mountains she writes about. She can often be found with her toes in the lake and a glass of wine in her hand, dreaming up her next book and working on her own happily ever after.

To learn more about Elena:
www.elenaaitken.com
elena@elenaaitken.com

Made in the USA
Las Vegas, NV
19 September 2024

95484827R00113